Text Classics

OLGA MASTERS was born in Pambula, on the far south coast of New South Wales, in 1919. Her first job, at seventeen, was at a local newspaper, where the editor encouraged her writing. She married at twenty-one and had seven children, working part-time as a journalist for papers such as the *Sydney Morning Herald*, leaving her little opportunity to develop her interest in writing fiction until she was in her fifties.

In the 1970s Masters wrote a radio play and a stage play, and between 1977 and 1981 she won a series of prizes for her short stories. Her debut collection, *The Home Girls*, won a National Book Council Award in 1983. It was followed by a novel, *Loving Daughters*, which was highly commended for the same award. Her next books, the linked stories *A Long Time Dying* and the novel *Amy's Children*, met with critical acclaim. This brief but highly prolific period ended when Masters died, following a short illness, in 1986. She had been at work on *The Rose Fancier*, a posthumously published collection of stories.

Reporting Home, a selection of Masters' extensive journalism, was published in 1990. A street in Canberra bears her name.

GEORDIE WILLIAMSON has been the *Australian*'s chief literary critic since 2008. He won the 2011 Pascall Prize for criticism and his book *The Burning Library* will be published soon by Text.

ALSO BY OLGA MASTERS

Loving Daughters
A Long Time Dying (stories)
Amy's Children
The Rose Fancier (stories)

Non-fiction
Reporting Home (ed. Deirdre Coleman)

The Home Girls
Olga Masters

Text Publishing Melbourne Australia

textclassics.com.au
textpublishing.com.au

The Text Publishing Company
Swann House
22 William Street
Melbourne Victoria 3000
Australia

First published by University of Queensland Press 1982
This edition published by The Text Publishing Company 2012

Some of these stories have been published before: 'Call Me Pinkie' and 'Adams
and Barker' in the *Sydney Morning Herald*; 'A Young Man's Fancy' in *Stories
of Her Life*, ed. Sandra Zurbo (Outback Press, 1979); 'A Good Marriage' in
South Pacific Stories, ed. Chris and Helen Tiffin (South Pacific Association for
Commonwealth Literature and Language Studies, 1980); 'You'll Like It There'
has been broadcast by Radio 5UV Adelaide.

Cover design by WH Chong
Page design by Text
Typeset by Midland Typesetters

Printed in Australia by Griffin Press, an Accredited ISO AS/NZS 14001:2004
Environmental Management System printer

Primary print ISBN: 9781922079466
Ebook ISBN: 9781921961748
Author: Masters, Olga, 1919-1986.
Title: The home girls / Olga Masters ; introduction by Geordie Williamson.
Series: Text classics.
Other Authors/Contributors: Williamson, Geordie.
Dewey Number: A823.3

CONTENTS

INTRODUCTION
An Ever More Polished Plainness
by Geordie Williamson
VII

Home Girls
XV

The Home Girls   1
The Rages of Mrs Torrens   12
On the Train   29
Leaving Home   36
Passenger to Berrigo   56
The Done Thing   74
A Rat in the Building   96
A Dog that Squeaked   114
A Young Man's Fancy   125
The Lang Women   139
The Snake and Bad Tom   160
A Poor Winner   170
Call Me Pinkie   179
Adams and Barker   187
Mrs Lister   198
The Creek Way   209
The Children Are Coming   229
A Good Marriage   251
You'll Like It There   267
The Sea on a Sunday   277

An Ever More
Polished Plainness
by Geordie Williamson

IF you know one thing about Olga Masters it will likely be that her first book, a collection of short stories called *The Home Girls*, was published when she was sixty-three. Her literary career lasted just six years after that, concluding with an unfinished collection of short fiction, *The Rose Fancier*, published two years after her death in 1986 from a brain tumour. Two novels, a play, a radio drama and fifty-four stories, many of which are no longer than a few pages, comprise almost all of Masters' output. On this slender body of work hangs one of the truly substantial reputations in contemporary Australian literature.

Les Murray was among the first to note the special quality of her fiction. He encouraged her to submit two early stories to the *Sydney Morning Herald* in

1979, one of which, 'Call Me Pinkie', was published in the paper. After Masters shared a major short-story prize in 1980 with Elizabeth Jolley the University of Queensland Press, publishers of Peter Carey and David Malouf, commissioned her first collection and went on to publish all her work. Critics, academics and fellow writers were unstinting in their praise. It was a matter for general wonder that a writer of such gifts should have chosen to raise a large family before starting to write.

As always, the truth is more complicated. Masters, who was born in 1919 and raised on the New South Wales south coast, actually published her first two stories in 1934. They appeared in the *Cobargo Chronicle*, a local newspaper where Masters worked briefly as a gopher during the worst years of the Depression, until the editor was unable to meet even the modest cost of keeping her on. Slight and derivative though they were, the pieces were remarkable efforts for a girl whose formal education ceased at fifteen, and who was the second of eight children from an impoverished rural household. In her 1991 biography of the writer, Julie Lewis reports that Masters' reading material during those years was the newssheets used to wrap the groceries.

Nor did Masters wait for her family to grow up before returning to writing. She was thirty-five, the wife of a country headmaster and a mother of six when domestic life and small-town society got the better of her, and she returned to journalism. Working as a stringer for various local papers she covered weddings and tea parties, concerts and school news: the women's round. This was the beginning of a long apprenticeship in drawing narrative sustenance from niggardly stores. As Masters explained in a 1986 interview with Jennifer Ellison: 'I learned a lot about human nature, and human behaviour, as a journalist. I worked on small papers and you'd go out for a story and it wouldn't be much of a story, but you'd make it into a story. The lesson there was that there is more in life, more in situations, than meets the eye. The deeper you dig, the more you find.'

This, too, is the collective lesson of Olga Masters' fiction. Her short stories and novels suggest that passion or violence need not be external, a matter of the public or political, but may be internalised instead—lodged deep within the human heart. Her fictions seem so humble in conception, so soothing in domestic scope, that their ferocity comes as a shock. The classical order of Masters' literary forms and the tidy language she employs don't disguise the potential for anarchy in ordinary life; instead, they clarify its possibility, just as the neatness of an obsessive-compulsive admits the disorder to which objects are prone.

Masters' fictions are mostly set far from the flourishing present: on hardscrabble smallholdings and pastoral concerns, in village cottages and inner-city terraces. They take as their background the Great War's aftermath, the biting Depression years, the vast disruptions of World War II and the creeping modernity that followed in its wake. They span an era in which poverty or loss deforms the lives of individuals, families and entire communities; when isolation, both literal and psychological, can be so total as to turn those who suffer its effects into fantasists and schizoids. In this world, men's unwillingness or inability to communicate is a perquisite of gender, and women variously exhibit what a philosopher once called 'the terrible power of the oppressed'. Here children, cast early into adult responsibility, seem closer to vassals than daughters or sons.

Yet, for all the unspoken misery of their inner lives, the rigid roles and petty strictures that govern their days, Masters' characters have authentic relations with all around them. Their engagement with reality is unmediated by pop psychology or mass media. It has a purity that bathes even the worst acts in an innocent light. To recognise this aspect of Masters' vision is not to engage in nostalgia for lost virtues—though the men and women she describes have all but passed from the typology of Australian selves—rather, it is to accept the narrow and superannuated character of her creations as a necessary attribute of their enduring worth. The child of rural poverty raised in the 1920s and '30s in a distant corner of New South Wales, and the young woman who escaped to the city only to find herself pulled back to the bush as a wife and mother at the mercy of her husband's career, did as Chekhov instructed and passed judgement on what she knew best.

A single story from *The Home Girls* can serve as a fractal image of the larger patterns in Masters' work. 'The Rages of Mrs Torrens' is set in Tantello—'a town with a sawmill, some clusters of grey unpainted weatherboard cottages, a hall and the required number of shops for a population of two hundred'. The story blends aspects of her personal geography (the name of the town is a portmanteau of Tanto and Candelo, two south coast towns where she lived as a child, though the tale is actually set north of Sydney) and personal history (Mrs Torrens was partly modelled on a woman Masters knew). Masters' fiction often draws on real places, persons and events, but its focus is so tight that only the foreground remains in the picture—reality becomes a blur at the edges of her art.

The narrative, which unfolds in the warm earth tones of extended anecdote, tells of a mill worker's wife whose temper is so intense—volcanically unpredictable and unusual in expression—that passing on her latest outrage has become the town's unofficial sport. There is the day that Mrs Torrens and a car filled with her thrilled and terrified children leap a partially repaired bridge, Dukes of Hazzard style. And there is the night when, for reasons unknown, she scatters two pounds of shilling pieces, her husband Harold's much-needed pay, into the icy creek behind their rented home.

While moods so extreme amount to a kind of social Tourette's, Masters does not describe them in clinical terms. From the outside (and we, as readers, often learn of events via the recycled rumours of the townsfolk), Mrs Torrens' anger could be mistaken for the protests of an independent and exuberantly sensual woman who finds herself trapped in the open-air confines of an Australian country town.

Crisis comes when Harold accidentally loses his right hand to a milling blade. Soon after, a still and erect Mrs Torrens appears at his workplace to confront the mill staff, who are visibly nervous—and with reason, as Mrs Torrens' reaction is to arm herself with a length of timber and lay waste to the office tea room, smashing china cups and sending the primus stove 'like a flaming ball bowling across the floor'.

But these violent acts are not what make the account so strange; it is what accompanies them. Masters lingers over Mrs Torrens' clothing, describing 'a black dress with a scarf-like trimming from one shoulder trailing to her waist': 'On the end she had pinned clusters of red geraniums and on her head she wore a large brimmed black hat with more geraniums tucked into the band of faded ribbon. On her feet she wore old sandshoes with the laces gone.'

The ensemble's final effect may be eccentric, but it is not insane. There is a feminine challenge in this

homemade glamour. In the moments before her vandal-
ism Mrs Torrens clambers up a pile of sawn timber
and onto a high fence, where she performs a defiant
dance above the assembled eyes of the men. 'What
have you done with my beautiful, beautiful manikin?'
is her sing-song question, addressed to everyone and
no one. They are the only words she utters throughout.

In days to come the dance will prove more troubling
to those mill workers than any broken china: 'Some
repeated her words but kept them inside their throats in
the darkness of their bedrooms and seizing their wives
for lovemaking held onto the vision of Mrs Torrens with
her still face under her black hat and her strong thighs
moving under her black dress as she walked the fence.'

The 'rage that ended all the rages of Mrs Torrens
in Tantello' is not the story's conclusion. We learn
of the family's subsequent flight to the city and the
adult Torrens' years of working together as cleaners—
she his literal right hand—of the final taming of her
temper with the aid of medication, and of her death,
in her fifties, from a heart attack. The story ends with
her daughter Aileen, now a successful clothes designer
(her mother's sartorial extravagance normalised into
an occupation), passing through Tantello on a whim
during her honeymoon and stopping by her former
home, which has fallen into ruin.

In its folkloric dramatisation of small-town comm-
unity, its celebration of the power of female sexuality

and its nursery-rhyme rhythms, 'The Rages of Mrs Torrens' is extraordinary. The rapid movement of the tale subverts its realism, while the minimal punctuation common to all Masters' early stories lends artlessness to what is an otherwise tightly composed work.

Toughness, humour, irony, sympathy for outsiders, as well as for mothers and daughters: these are the base elements of Olga Masters' fiction. And in the few years left to her after *The Home Girls* Masters worked tirelessly to refine them, eventually achieving a style as straightforward as her psychology was complex. Her curious achievement was an ever more polished plainness: a simplicity of tone that honoured the modesty of the subjects it described.

When Masters died, in September 1986, she was still working on her final short-story collection, *The Rose Fancier.* The title story is the last in the volume, as the author intended, and it is one of eight to exist in a final-draft state. In it a country solicitor of the Edwardian era sets aside a quarter-acre of his garden for roses, and as the bushes grow and spread he removes the stakes that hold them. As a valedictory emblem for Masters' stories they are marvellously apt: all issue from the same dark soil of the author's experience but burgeon in the many colours of her imagination. Readers should beware, however: hidden in the beauty of their telling are points that wound; there are real thorns in her imaginary gardens.

The Home Girls

For Alice

"It's today," the fat child said and rolled over in bed landed on her feet on the floor and held the window sill, looking back at her sister, the thin one who had been jerked awake.

"Today!" the fat one said.

The thin one half raised herself on her elbows in bed. Her straight hair fell over her face. The fat one had curly hair in corkscrews over her head.

"Should be the other way round," a visitor said once, looking at them with a stretched mouth and blank eyes.

The visitor meant that straight hair would have taken away from the fat one's rounded look and curls might have made the thin one look rounder.

The foster mother looked at them not bothering to stretch her mouth.

The fat one and the thin one looked away not knowing how to apologize for being the way they were.

"Go and play," the foster mother said, but they were already going.

The fat one picked up a brush now and pressed it down her curls which sprang back in the wake of the bristles.

When she put the brush down she saw in the mirror her hair was the same as before.

The thin one screwed her body so that she could see the fat one's reflection. "Are you?" she said.

"Am I what?" the fat one answered.

"You know." The thin one moved a foot which need not have belonged to her body so flat were the bedclothes. "Excited about it," the thin one said.

"Yes!" said the fat one, too loud and too sudden.

Tears came into the thin one's eyes. "Don't shout!" she said.

The fat one picked up the brush and began to drag at her curls again. The thin one's watery eyes met her sister's in the mirror. They looked like portraits on a mantlepiece, the subjects photographed while the tension was still in their expression.

The foster mother came into the room then. She made the third portrait on the mantlepiece.

The thin one started to get out of bed rather quickly. Her ears were ready for the orders so she began to pull blankets off for the bedmaking.

But the foster mother said, "Leave that."

The thin one didn't know what to do then. She thrust a finger up her nose and screwed it round.

The foster mother covered her face with both hands. After a while she took them away showing a stretched mouth.

"Now!" she said quite brightly looking between them.

Now what? thought the fat one and the thin one.

Their mouths hung a little open.

The foster mother squeezed her eyes shut.

When she opened them the fat one and the thin one were in the same pose.

She crossed to the window and raised the blind quite violently.

"Have you had your bath?" she said.

They knew she knew they hadn't because it was there on the back of her neck.

She turned abruptly and went out of the room.

They heard her angry heels on the stairs.

The fat one bent down and opened a drawer. It was empty.

"Our clothes?" she said.

The thin one stared at a suitcase fastened and strapped standing upright in a corner.

"They're all in there," the fat one said, pointing.

"Take something out to wear," the thin one said making a space on the bed for the case.

Inside the clothes were in perfect order, a line of dresses folded with the tops showing, a stack of pants, a corner filled with rolled up socks, nightgowns with the lace ironed, cardigans carefully buttoned.

The fat one's hands hovered over them.

"Which?" she said.

She touched the pants and they were soon screwed and tossed under her fingers.

"Stop!" said the thin one and slapped her sister's hand away.

She plucked up two pairs of pants and then put them back.

"Fold them the way she did!" the fat one said.

The thin one tried but couldn't.

"Let me!" said the fat one, but digging in she tossed a dress so that the folded underneath came to the top.

They looked around at a noise and the foster mother was there.

"Look what you've done!" she screamed and the fat one and the thin one flung themselves together away from the case on the bed.

They blinked as if blows were descending on them.

The foster mother turned her head towards the stairs.

"Hilda!" she cried, squashing her face against the door jamb.

4

The body of Hilda the foster mother's sister who came to the house every day jerked into sight, coming from the bottom of the stairs like an open mouthed fish swimming to the surface.

The foster mother now had both hands pressed to her face.

Shutting the fat one and the thin one out of her vision, Hilda went to the case and began to lift little bundles of clothes onto the bed.

"You go down and pour yourself a cup of tea," she said.

The foster mother's heels went down again, thudding dully this time.

"Go and have your bath," Hilda said, her eyes on the folding and the packing.

They went into the bathroom off the landing.

There hanging on the shower rail were the clothes they were to wear. The dresses were on hangers, pants and vests and socks were folded over the rail.

Shoes polished to a high gloss were on a bathroom chair.

"She told us last night," the thin one said.

The fat one's face remembered.

Very slow and deliberate she turned the water on.

She stared at it rushing away without the plug in.

The thin one sat on the toilet seat and began to pull on her socks.

The fat one too dressed slowly.

Before she put her pants on she turned around flicked up her skirt and urinated in the bath.

It trickled down to join the rushing water.

Thoughtfully she turned the tap off.

They stood in the silence staring about them.

The hard white shining walls stared back.

"Look!" said the thin one suddenly taking a lipstick from a little ceramic bowlful on a ledge below a cabinet. The foster mother kept them there sometimes using the bathroom to freshen up after housecleaning.

The thin one uncapped and screwed the metal holder sending the scarlet worm out like a living thing.

The fat one also took a lipstick out of the bowl.

She laughed when hers was longer and a shade more scarlet.

They looked in the mirror and saw not their own reflection but that of the foster mother bracing her jaws and pulling her lips back her cold watery eyes shutting out everything but her own image.

The fat one turned and leaned across the bath with the lipstick poised.

Her eyes flashing briefly on the thin one said what she would do.

Her pink tongue, shaped like the lipstick end, showed at the corner of her mouth.

She braced herself against the wall with a spread plump hand.

6

The lipstick cut deep into the wall sprinkling a few scarlet crumbs.

The fat one wrote her word.

Shithead.

The thin one made a little noise of breathing. She leaned over beside her sister. She was slower and her tongue was out further.

She wrote *cock*.

The fat one made a small noise of scorn.

She took a step level with a piece of virgin wall.

She wrote *fuck*.

The thin one wrote with the letters going downwards.

Piss.

She broke her lipstick when she dotted the *i*.

The piece fell into the bath. The fat one laughed and ground it into the porcelain wiping her shoe on the side of the tub.

Then she climbed onto the side of the bath. High above the words she began to draw.

It was a penis so big she wore the lipstick down to the metal holder when she finished.

The thin one climbed up beside her. She drew a cascade of little circles falling from the tip of the penis, the last unfinished because her lipstick stump gave out.

They jumped down together, the fat one light like a pillow and the thin one bending her knees and creaking when she landed.

7

They dropped the lipstick holders on the floor and watched them roll away.

The door opened then and Hilda was there.

All that moved was the hair sprouting from a mole at the corner of her mouth.

"Oh my God," she said at last.

Then she breathed in raising her bosom and crossing both hands near her throat.

The fat one and the thin one jerked their smeared hands away from their stiffly ironed dresses.

"My God," said Hilda, able to look at them now. "I'd kill you if I had you."

"Yes," said the fat one and the thin one sounding as if they'd heard it before.

Hilda flashed open a cabinet and took out a cake of grey gritty soap and dropped it in the basin.

"Scrub your hands with that," she said.

They did standing back with spread out legs to keep splashes off their clothes.

Hilda was ready with a soiled towel fished from the linen basket.

"She did everything in her power for you," she said in a deep and trembling voice. "Out of the goodness of her heart she did every single thing she could."

The fat one and the thin one didn't know what to do with the towel when they had finished wiping, but Hilda seized it and flung it into the basket.

"Carry your case down," she said going ahead of them.

Halfway down the stairs they came in view of the heads.

The foster mother and a man and a woman were standing around looking up.

The foster mother's mouth was stretched in one of her smiles.

"Your new mother and father have come to collect you. Isn't that nice?" she said in a gay voice.

"We're carrying you off before breakfast," said the woman nearly as gay.

"Hilda, whip out into the kitchen and get some apples to chew on the way," said the foster mother.

Hilda slipped past the group. The fat one and the thin one watched but the backs of her legs did not speak.

The woman took a hand of each. She rubbed a thumb on each palm wondering briefly at the cool and gritty feel.

"You'll have four brothers and sisters at the cottage," she said.

"Cottage," said the foster mother. "Doesn't that sound cosy?"

Hilda returned putting the apples into a paper bag.

The man picked up the case and everyone moved to the car parked near the porch.

The fat one and the thin one got in quickly and each sat in a corner of the back seat wriggling until the leather clutched them.

The foster mother put her face to the half wound up window.

"Write us a little letter about how you're getting on," she said.

When the car moved off she kissed the tips of her fingers to them.

Four brothers and sisters, the fat one and the thin one were thinking.

At that moment the foster mother being shown the bathroom by Hilda was clutching her sister and saying Oh my God, oh my God, oh my God, over and over.

The fat one and the thin one weren't remembering it at all.

We lived in this beautiful house with our own bathroom, the fat one said to herself seeing in her mind four pairs of entranced eyes.

The car swerved suddenly to miss an overtaking lorry.

The man swore and the woman put a hand on his arm to restrain him turning her head to see if the back had heard.

There was this terrible accident killing our father and mother, the thin one said silently to her imaginary audience.

Lapsed into their dream the fat one pulled at her corkscrew curls and the thin one twisted the ends of her hair and they watched for the cottage to come into view.

The rages of Mrs Torrens kept the town of Tantello constantly in gossip.

Or more accurately in constant entertainment.

It was a town with a sawmill, some clusters of grey unpainted weatherboard cottages, a hall and the required number of shops for a population of two hundred.

Even while Mrs Torrens was having a temporary lull from one of her rages the subject was not similarly affected.

"How's the wife these days?" a mill worker would say to Harold while they shovelled a path through the sawdust for a lorry.

The man's eyes would not meet Harold's but slide away.

Remarks like this would be made when life was more than usually dull in Tantello, for example during the long spell between the sports day in midwinter and the Christmas tree in December.

A mill wife having seen Mrs Torrens behaving like other mill wives in Tantello that day would suggest while chopping up her meat for stew or melon for jam that Kathleen may never have another of her rages.

It was not said hopefully though just dutifully.

It took some time for Tantello to settle down after the rage that sent Mrs Torrens and the five little Torrenses flying over the partly-built bridge across Tantello Creek.

The barrier at the finished end was down so Mrs Torrens one of the few women in Tantello who drove a car ripped across towards the gaping workmen standing with crowbars and other tools.

"Whee-eee-eee!" they called as they flung themselves out of her way clinging to the rails while she flung the old Ford across, sending the temporary wooden planks on the gaping floor sliding dangerously and landing the car on the gravel bridge approach.

It paused a second with the workmen expecting it to dive backwards into the creek, then with a groan negotiated the little ridge with the back wheels spitting stones and dust.

A little Torrens screamed in ecstasy (or relief) and standing behind her mother scooped up handfuls of Kathleen's magnificent red hair and laid her face in it.

"Stop that!" cried another little Torrens beside her. "Mumma can't drive the car properly if you do that!"

The little Torrenses told their father this and Harold although not often moved to do so repeated the remark to the mill hands and for weeks afterwards Tantello feasted on it.

"Mumma can't drive the car properly if you do that!" they chuckled over and over above the screams of the machinery cutting timber, not always seeing each other clearly through the smoke from the smouldering sawdust.

"How many stories have you got Dad, on Raging Torrens?" asked a little Cleary one night from the floor where he was doing his homework.

He was Thomas Cleary, aged eleven, and Thomas senior, when there were no fresh stories on the rages of Mrs Torrens to relate or repeat, boasted to the mill hands on the cleverness of his son and his promising future.

"Head stuck in a book all day long," Thomas senior would say disregarding the predictions of other workers that he would end up in the mill like most other youth of Tantello.

Seated by the stove fire now Thomas senior burst into proud laughter at this fresh evidence of his son's calculating mind and whispered the sentence to have it right to tell at the mill next day.

"How many stories have you got on Raging Torrens?" he whispered into the fire averting his face so that his wife would not see.

Thomas and Evelyn Cleary no longer shared anything. She was a stout plain woman with a lot of hair on her face who pulled her mouth down at most things Thomas said. The day before Thomas had brought home a gift of turnips from a fellow mill hand but Mrs Cleary threw them to the fowls declaring they gave her wind.

"Now the eggs'll give you wind," said Thomas but the little Clearys did not laugh with him because they sided with the stronger of their parents in the uncanny way children have of defining where their fortunes lie.

As far as the stories on Raging Torrens or Roaring Kathleen went there were too many to list here.

There was the time when she charged out at midnight and flung Harold's pay in the creek.

It was an icy July night with a brilliant moon and when the catastrophe was discovered all the Torrenses went to the creek to try and recover the two pounds in two shilling pieces.

"Oh, Harold I must be mad," moaned Mrs Torrens thigh deep in water groping around a rock and coming up mostly with flat stones.

(Harold did not tell the mill hands this.)

"My little ones'll die of pneumonia!" she cried, "Oh my little Dollikins, forgive your wicked Mumma!"

Harold had to rise at four o'clock next morning for an early shift so it was he who said they should go home.

"What will we eat now?" murmured a little Torrens old enough to understand the simple economics of life, like passing money across the counter of Bert Herbert's store before goods were passed back.

"Oh, Harold," moaned Mrs Torrens, "We can't even make a pot of tea. There'll by none for tomorrow if we do!"

"O, my poor mannikin! You can't go to work with your innards as dry as the scales on a goanna's back!"

She stood in the glow of the stove fire which Harold had got going among the little Torrenses all crouched over it. Her nightgown slipped from her shoulders showing her white neck threaded with blue veins. Her red hair wet from her wet hands was strewn about and her blue eyes welled with tears. Harold stood staring long at her and the little Torrenses looked from him to their mother and back into the heart of the glowing stove. In a little while without anyone speaking they scurried off to bed.

Kathleen rubbed one icy foot upon the other clutching a threadbare towel about her waist under her nightie to rub dry her icy thighs and buttocks.

"Lie down on the floor close to the fire," whispered Harold. "And afterwards I'll rub you warm again."

"Of course," she whispered back and sinking down reached up both arms to him.

When the pain of the loss of Harold's pay had eased it actually became a subject for discussion. Gathered around the meal table the Torrenses talked about what the two pounds would have bought.

"Pounds and pounds of butter!" cried a little Torrens whose teeth marks were embedded in a slice of bread spread with grey dripping.

"How many pounds then?" asked Harold. "How much is butter? One and threepence? How many pounds in two pounds? Come on, work it out! Thomas Cleary could!"

"What else would it have bought Mumma and Dadda?" cried the seven year old Torrens.

"Tinned peaches, jelly, fried sausages!" screeched her sister.

"Blankets! One for each of our beds!" cried Mrs Torrens unable to contain herself.

Then she dropped her face on her hand and shook her hair down to cover her lowered eyes and dripping tears.

"A new coat with fur on it for Mumma!" said an observing little Torrens.

Kathleen lifted her head and shook back her hair.

"I like my old coat best!" she said.

"See," said Harold clasping his wife's hands. "Mumma doesn't want a new coat. So the money was no use to us after all!"

Although this deduction puzzled some of the little Torrenses they were happy to see their mother smiling and ecstatic when she flung her head towards Harold and fitted it into the curve of his neck and shoulder.

They trooped outside to play soon after.

The creek figured in many of the rages of Mrs Torrens particularly her milder ones.

When in one of these she took the children to picnic just below the bridge on a Sunday afternoon.

The normal Tantello people considered this the height of eccentricity, the place for Sunday picnics being the beach twenty-five miles away available to those with reliable cars, and for the others there was the annual outing with the townspeople packed into three timber trucks.

Tantello Creek was a wide bed of sand with only a trickle of water in most parts, but there was a sandbank a few yards upstream from the bridge with a miniature waterfall and a chain of water holes, most of them small and shallow petering out as they moved towards the main stream.

This is where Mrs Torrens took the children for a picnic in full view of Tantello taking Sunday afternoon walks across the bridge.

Mrs Torrens spread out the bread and jam and watercress gathered by the children and they ate on the green slope below the road with an occasional car passing in line with their heads and the walking Tantello staring from the bridge.

"Go home you little parlingtons and stop staring!" cried Mrs Torrens waving a thick wedge of bread towards the bridge.

"Are you swearing at us, Mrs Torrens?" said one of the starers.

"You know swearing when you hear it! Or do you plug your ears after closing times on Saturday when your Pa comes home?"

"Oh, Mumma," breathed an agonized Torrens named Aileen, the eldest of the family.

She shared a seat at school with the group on the bridge.

Aileen left the picnic then and moved with head down towards the water.

"Only mad people make up words," called a daring voice from the bridge.

Aileen lowered her head further in the silence following.

Mrs Torrens jumped to her feet to herd the little Torrenses to the water to join their sister.

"We'll gather our stones and hold them under the water!" she cried and the little Torrenses with the exception of Aileen dispersed to hunt for flat round stones that changed colour on contact with the running water.

The little Torrenses watched spellbound when the stones emerged wet and glistening and streaked with oche red, rich browns, soft blues and greys and sometimes pale gold.

"Oh don't go dull!" screamed the little Torrenses hoping for a miracle to save the colours from merging into a dull stone colour when the water dried.

Aileen some distance away dug her toes into the sand and stared down at them. Her lashes lay soft as brown bracken fern on her apricot cheeks.

"Come on Snobbie Dobbie!" called Mrs Torrens.

"Come and wash the beautiful stones and see the colours!

"They're brown and beautiful as your eyes, Snobbie Dobbie!"

"Come on, come on!" called the other little Torrenses.

In the end Aileen came and the high voices and peals of laughter from the creek bed had the effect of sending the walking Tantello mooching home across the bridge.

There came the rage that ended all the rages of Mrs Torrens in Tantello and drove the family from the town.

Harold lost the fingers of his right hand in a mill accident.

Holding a length of timber against a screaming saw, a drift of smoke blew across his eyes and the saw made a raw and ugly stump of his hand and the blood rushed over the saw teeth and down the arm of his old striped shirt and the yelling of the mill hands brought the work to a halt and for a moment all was still except the damaging drift of smoke from a sawdust fire.

A foreman with a knowledge of first aid (for many fingers were lost at the mill although Harold was the first to lose all four) stopped the flow of blood and drove Harold twenty miles to the nearest hospital.

When the mill was silenced an hour before the midday break the townspeople sensed something was wrong and Mrs Torrens came running too.

A chain of faces turned and passed the word along that it was Harold. Mrs Torrens stood still and erect strangely dressed in a black dress with a scarf-like trimming from one shoulder trailing to her waist. On the end she had pinned clusters of red geraniums and on her head she wore a large brimmed black hat with more geraniums tucked into the band of faded ribbon. On her feet she wore old sandshoes with the laces gone.

All the eyes of the watching Tantello were fixed on Mrs Torrens who stood a little apart. She stared back with a tilted chin and wide and cold blue eyes until they turned away and one by one left the scene. When the last had gone she walked into the mill to the cluster of men around the door of the small detached office.

"We're sorry, Mrs Torrens," said one of them.

Behind the men was a table with cups on it for the bosses' dinner and a kettle set on a primus stove. Mrs Torrens looked from the cups to the men's hands and back to the cups and a strange, small smile lit on her face.

Then she stalked to the timber stacked against the fence and climbed with amazing lightness and agility for a big woman onto it stepping up until her waist was level with the top of the fence. The men watched in fascination while she hauled herself onto the fence top and stood there balancing like a great black bird.

Her old sandshoes clinging to the fence top were like scruffy grey birds.

"Come down! We don't want no more accidents," called the mill owner.

But Mrs Torrens walked one panel with her arms out to balance herself. Then satisfied she was at home she straightened up and walked back, coming to a halt at the fence post and standing there looking down on the men whose faces were tipped up like eggs towards her.

She stared long at them.

"What have you done to my mannikin?" she said.

They were silent.

"My beautiful, beautiful mannikin?" she said slightly shaking her head.

"Accidents happen," said a foreman a small and shrivelled man who wet his lips and looked at the boss for approval in making his statement.

Mrs Torrens walked like a trapeze artist along the fence top to reach the other post.

She swooped once or twice to the left and the right and when she settled herself on the post she lifted her chin and adjusted her hat.

The foreman encouraged by the success of his earlier remark wet his lips again.

"Go home to your kiddies, Mrs Torrens," he said. "They need you at home."

He considered this well worth repeating in the hotel after work.

Mrs Torrens stared dreamily down on the men giving her head another little shake.

"My beautiful, beautiful mannikin," she said.

Then she put out both arms and almost ran to the other post laughing a little when she reached there safely.

Someone had lit the primus stove and the shrill whistle of the boiling kettle broke the silence causing everyone except Mrs Torrens to start.

She merely lowered herself and jumped lightly onto the timber picking her way down until she reached the ground. She shook the sawdust from her old sandshoes as if they were expensive and elegant footwear.

Then she looked about her moving pieces of timber with her foot until she found a shortish piece she could easily grip.

She then walked into the office and swung it back and forth among the things on the table sending the primus like a flaming ball bowling across the floor and pieces of china flying everywhere.

The men were galvanized into action beating at the blaze with bags jumping out of the way of the stream

23

of boiling water and trying vainly to save the cups and avoid contact with the timber wielded by Mrs Torrens.

After a while she threw her weapon among the debris and stalked off walking lightly casually through the mill gate and up the hill to where the Torrens house was. The little Torrenses home from school for midday dinner stood about with tragic expressions. Mrs Torrens broke into a brilliant smile.

"All of us will be Dadda's right hand now!" she called. "Dadda will have six right hands!"

She went ahead of them into the house.

"My beautiful, beautiful mannikin," she said.

It may seem strange but that, the most violent of all the rages of Mrs Torrens, was not generally discussed in Tantello.

Mill wives standing on verandahs and at windows saw her walk the fence and saw she spoke but the husbands evaded the questions on what was said.

Some repeated her words but kept them inside their throats in the darkness of their bedrooms and seizing their wives for lovemaking held onto the vision of Mrs Torrens with her still face under her black hat and her strong thighs moving under her black dress as she walked the fence.

Even Thomas Cleary couldn't be persuaded to repeat what Mrs Torrens said.

Young Thomas tried from the kitchen floor where he was doing his homework.

"What did Rager say, Dad?" said young Thomas. "What was she saying when she walked the fence top?"

"Don't you get ideas about walking the fence top," said Mrs Cleary from the table where she was sullenly making Thomas senior's lunch for the morrow. "Don't you go copying that crazy woman!"

Thomas senior jerked his head up and opened his mouth but closed it before a denial escaped his lips.

"Go on Dad! You musta heard Rager!" said young Thomas.

But Thomas senior staring into the scarlet stove fire saw only the flaming red of Mrs Torrens's hair and when a coal broke it seemed like the petals of red geraniums scattering into the ashes. He opened and closed his two good hands on his knees but even that did not ease the hunger inside him.

The Torrenses left Tantello soon after the accident. The townspeople let the family go without ceremony fearful that an appearance of support might jeopardize others' jobs at the mill.

The Torrenses left their furniture to sell for the rent they owed (for they never caught up from the week Kathleen threw Harold's pay into the creek) and took their clothing and what else could be stowed in the car besides the five children.

Mrs Torrens drove with Harold's useless heavily bandaged hand beside her.

She did in effect become his right hand.

25

The work they ultimately found in the city was cleaning a factory in two shifts a day, early morning and late afternoon.

Harold learned to wield a broom holding the handle in the crook of his right arm and Kathleen worked beside him picking up the rubbish he missed.

After some practice he was proficient and she could work independently so that they sometimes had time to sit on an upturned box and eat their sandwiches together Harold laying his on his knee between bites and holding his mug of tea with his left hand.

The rages of Mrs Torrens subsided with the help of medication from a public hospital not far from where they lived.

During these times Mrs Torrens's blue eyes dulled and her beautiful red hair straightened and she moved slowly and heavily with no life in her step or on her face.

She looked like a lot of the women in Tantello.

The little Torrenses did very well which would have amazed the people of Tantello if they had followed their fortunes in professions and trades.

Mrs Torrens was in her fifties when she died from a heart attack and Harold made his home with the second daughter Rachel who was a nurse educator in a big hospital with a flat of her own.

It was Aileen who won some modest fame in the rag trade.

She started sweeping floors and picking up pins and scraps of cloth then graduated to more important things.

When she was a beautiful young woman nearing thirty she was designing her own materials and having them made up into styles she created.

Long pursued by a colleague who designed and cut clothes for men she eventually married him and he agreed to her whim to drive through Tantello while on their honeymoon.

"Did you live here?" he said standing with her near the little grey house with the small square verandah now with all the railings missing and the roof on one side dipping dangerously over a tank tilted dangerously too from the half rotted tank stand.

She stood near a clump of red geraniums cold and proud and still as Kathleen stood outside the mill the day Harold lost his fingers.

"I lived here," she said and looked down on Tantello with the mill shut down now and only a few of the houses occupied mostly by Aboriginal families.

"Is that bridge safe to cross?" her husband asked looking at her profile with her lashes lying soft as brown bracken fern on her apricot cheeks.

She stretched her mouth in a smile he didn't understand and began to walk with Kathleen's walk light and casual towards the car.

He was a little ahead and his heart leapt when her heard her speak.

"My beautiful, beautiful mannikin," she said low and passionate.

He turned swiftly to take her hand.

Then he saw her face and felt he shouldn't.

The young woman not more than twenty-seven slammed the gate on herself and the two children both girls.

She did not move off at once but looked up and down the street as if deciding which way to go.

The older girl looked up at her through her hair which was whipped by the wind to read the decision the moment she made it.

Finally the woman took a hand of each child and turned in the direction of the railway station.

"Oh goody!" cried Sara who was nearly five.

"The sun's out," the woman murmured lifting her face up for a second towards it.

Sara looked again into her mother's face noticing two or three of her teeth pinning down her bottom lip and the glint in her eyes perhaps from the sun? She felt inadequate that she seldom noticed such things as sun and wind, barely bothering about the rain as well, being quite content to stay out and play in it. The weather appeared to figure largely in the lives of adults. Sara hoped this would work out for her when she was older.

The mother bent forward as she hurried the younger child Lisa having difficulty keeping up. Her face Sara saw looked strained like the mother's. Sara hoped she wouldn't complain. The glint in the mother's eyes was like a spark that could ignite and involve them all.

She saw with relief the roof of the station jutting above the street but flashed her eyes away from the buildings still to be passed before they reached it.

The ticket office was protected by the jutting roof.

Sara was glad of the rest while her mother had her head inside the window and laid her cheek lightly against her rump clad in a blue demin skirt.

The business of buying tickets went on for a long time. Sara's eyes conveyed to Lisa her fear that the mother's top half had disappeared forever inside the window. She clutched her skirt to drag her out and opened her mouth to scream. Lisa saw and screamed for her.

The mother flung both arms down brushing a child off with each. They dared not touch her when she turned around and separated the tickets from change in her purse.

She snapped it shut and looked up and around in a distracted way as if to establish where she was.

It was Sara who went in front taking the narrow path squeezed between a high fence on one side and the station wall on the other. She swung her head around to see that her mother and Lisa were following her bouncy confident step.

On the platform waiting for the train the few other passengers looked at them.

Sara's dress was long and her hair was long and she was not dressed warmly enough.

The people especially a couple of elderly women noted Sara's light cotton dress with a deep flounce at the hem and Lisa's skimpy skirt and fawn tights. They looked at the mother's hands to see if there was a bag hanging from them with cardigans or jumpers in. But the mother carried nothing but a leather shoulder bag about as large as a large envelope and quite flat.

"She's warm enough herself," one of the women murmured to her companion with a sniff.

They watched them board the train noticing the mother did not turn her head when she stepped onto the platform. It was Sara who grasped the hand of Lisa and saw her safely on.

"Tsk, tisk," said the watching woman wishing she could meet the mother's eyes and glare her disapproval.

31

The mother took a single seat near the aisle and let Sara and Lisa find one together across from her.

Dear little soul, thought the passenger on the seat facing them seeing Sara's face suffused with pleasure at her small victory. Lisa had to wriggle her bony little rump with legs stuck out stiffly to get onto the seat.

Sara read the passenger's thoughts.

"She doesn't like you helping," she said.

This was almost too much for the passenger whose glance leapt towards the mother to share with her this piece of childish wisdom.

But the mother had her profile raised and her eyes slanted away towards the window. The skin spread over her cheekbones made the passenger think of pale honey spread on a slice of bread.

She's beautiful. The woman was surprised at herself for not having noticed it at once.

She returned her attention rather reluctantly to Sara and Lisa.

She searched their faces for some resemblance to the mother. Sara's was round with blue worried eyes under faint eyebrows. Lisa's was pale with a pinched look and blue veins at the edges of her eyebrows disappearing under a woollen cap with a ragged tassel that looked as if a kitten had wrestled with it.

The passenger thought they might look like their father putting him into a category unworthy of the handsome mother.

32

For the next twenty minutes the train alternated between a rocking tearing speed and dawdling within sight of one of the half dozen stations on the way to the city and the passenger alternated her attention between the girls and the mother although at times she indulged in a fancy that she was not their mother but someone minding them.

"I can move and your mummy sit here," she said to Sara with sudden inspiration.

I'll find out for sure.

Sara put her head against the seat back, tipping her face and closing her eyes with pink coming into her cheeks.

The passenger looked to Lisa for an answer and Lisa turned her eyes towards her mother seeing only her profile and the long peaked collar of her blouse lying on her honey coloured sweater.

Lisa looked into the passenger's face and gave her head the smallest shake.

Poor little soul.

The passenger stared at the mother knowing in the end she would look back.

The mother did her eyes widening for a second under bluish lids with only a little of her brow visible under a thick bang of fair hair. There was nothing friendly in her face.

The passenger reddened and looked at the girls.

"Your mummy's so pretty," she said.

Sara swung her head around to look at the mother and Lisa allowed herself a tiny smile as if it didn't need verification.

"Do you like having a pretty mummy?" the passenger asked.

The mother had turned her attention to the window again and her eyes had narrowed.

The passenger felt as if a door had been shut in her face.

"Are you going into the city for the day?" she said to the girls.

Sara pressed her lips together as if she shouldn't answer if she wanted to. Lisa's mouth opened losing its prettiness and turning into an uneven hole.

There's nothing attractive about either of them, thought the passenger deciding that Lisa might be slightly cross-eyed.

She sat with her handbag gripped on her knees and her red face flushed a deeper red and her brown eyes with flecks of red in the whites were flint-hard when they darted between the mother and the girls and vacant when they looked away.

After a moment the mother turned her head and stared into the passenger's face. The girls raised their eyes and looked too. The train swayed and rushed and all the eyes locked together. The mother's eyes although large and blue and without light were the snake's eyes mesmerizing those of the passenger. Sara swung her eyes from the passenger to the mother as if trying to protect one from the other. Lisa's face grew tight and white and she opened her small hole of a mouth but no sound came out.

The mother keeping her eyes on the passenger got up suddenly and checked the location through the window. Sara and Lisa stumbled into the aisle holding out frantic fingers but afraid to touch her.

Sara stood under her mother's rump as close as she dared her eyes turned back to see Lisa holding the seat end. The train swayed and clanged the last hundred yards slowing and sliding like a skier at the bottom of a snow peak stopping with a suddeness that flung Sara and Lisa together across the seat end.

This was fortunate.

The mother level with the passenger now leaned down and sparks from her eyes flew off the hard flat stones of the passenger's eyes.

"I'm going to kill them," the mother said.

There was a practice at Berrigo to gather at the Post Office in the afternoon to wait for the mail.

The doors closed while it was sorted and by the time they were ready to open a crowd swelled by children from both the public and Catholic school had filled the porch.

Weeks before Sylvia McMahon was to leave for Sydney to find a job she was singled out for attention when she arrived with the others to wait for the mail.

"Won't be long now," said Mrs Percy Parnell (there was also Mrs Henry and Mrs Horace) who as the youngest of the trio felt she had a licence to use current slang terms of which this was one.

Sylvia smiled, pleased at the attention focused on her.

"Three weeks," she said, feeling the old familiar tingle.

"And three and a half days," said her small sister Esme who blushed and hid her face in her sister's skirt when everyone laughed.

Esme aged ten amid the flock of schoolchildren could have collected the mail but Sylvia sixteen and waiting for departure day dressed herself like the adult women of Berrigo and went daily to the Post Office, probably to collect no more than a *Farmer and Settler* and a doctor's bill which Mrs McMahon would throw in the fire since she had not paid for the confinement resulting in Sylvia much less Frank, Lennie, Esme, Rose, Yvonne and Jackie.

It was true that Sylvia could have been employed helping her mother but the income from the farm was stretched to the limits, and it took a good season during which the cows gave liberally of their milk to atone for the bleak winter when grocery bills mounted month after month and unlike the doctor's bill could not be thrown into the stove and forgotten.

Mrs McMahon now past forty hoped for no more children and avoiding old Doctor Hadgett was relatively easy as he spent most of his time behind the high garden wall of his house and surgery within arm's reach of his liquor cupboard.

These days he was of little use in confinements anyway handing over to the district nurse when a birth was imminent and charging for the lavatory.

But it was a different matter in relation to the town's only grocer.

L.F. Parrington was a prominent local figure running the agricultural show and sports day or running the committee running the events. L.F. as the townspeople called him was churchman, sportsman, businessman and with one of the district's best farms. He was in everything and everywhere. You would have to be a recluse to dodge him. Mrs McMahon gave him the child endowment cheque each month in the winter and was grateful for the brief lift of his hat when their paths crossed.

Since no jobs were offering in Berrigo or larger towns within a radius of one hundred miles it was proposed that Sylvia go to Sydney before the winter set in and with luck get work. With a little more luck the pay might allow her to send some money home.

"Parcels too," said Sylvia at home after the post office jaunt and wiping up for her mother with a threadbare tea towel. The subject was invariably the going away.

She glanced at her mother seeing side-on the drooped eyelids and corresponding droop to the mouth still soft and pretty in spite of all the children and hard work.

Mrs McMahon had been silent while Sylvia rattled on. Now Sylvia saw something set and unyielding in her mother's profile.

"Things are so cheap in Sydney," Sylvia said.

Mrs McMahon spoke at last.

"You're not there yet," she said.

Sylvia laid down a plate in fear. Would it be possible her mother would change her mind and not let her go? She must know at once if there was a hint of this!

She stared hard at a handful of forks.

"Can we write and say the date I'll be there?" she said.

Oh, God don't let her say I can't go!

Mrs McMahon took the washing up dish and moved up a step onto the verandah tipping the contents onto flowers that grew below the rails.

Sylvia watched her back, heard the rush of water.

When she turns and shows her face I'll know, Sylvia thought entertaining the idea of rushing on her and begging her not to say no.

But the McMahons did not demonstrate affection and they kissed begrudgingly the children fearful of hearing the words "Don't slobber like a calf!"

Mrs McMahon kept her eyes down when she stepped back into the kitchen the dish under her arm.

"That's done," she said hanging it in its place above the fountain in the stove recess.

The recess and a door leading outside took up one end of the kitchen. Built of corrugated iron smoked grey-black the recess was big enough for both the stove and an iron grate for an open fire in the winter.

Sylvia saw herself sitting by it with the others on cold nights, her father taking most of the lamplight reading the *Farmer and Settler*, her mother in the shadows making who she called a "start for tomorrow" which was slicing bread for school sandwiches and soaking oatmeal for porridge.

A chill as cold as the coldest night ran through Sylvia. Would she be here this winter and the winters to come, all her life in Berrigo with no one decent to marry? Oh my God to end up a Gough, a Motbey, a Wright, a Henry or a Turner! To die would be better!

All her youth spent with no money of her own, no job but helping her mother around the house, nothing to go to but the Berrigo Show and the Berrigo Sports and the Agricultural Ball where Berrigo's idea of decoration was to pile the stage with potatoes, pumpkins and marrows and cross stalks of corn around the walls! You felt you were dancing in the farm sheds.

She sank onto a chair pushing her feet out before her and raising her eyes to see a piece of sky visible where the galvanized iron did not quite meet.

Oh to be free as the sky, to escape forever the closeting of the kitchen!

"Can't we write to Aunt Bess and say when I'll be coming?" she said staring at her skirt stretched tight across her knees.

40

Her mother was dragging the sewing machine to catch the late afternoon light from the one window and didn't hear or chose not to hear.

She sat at the machine and began to sort through a little pile of cutout garments still with the paper pattern against each piece.

My dress! thought Sylvia. She has been reminded to sew my dress! But Mrs McMahon bypassed Sylvia's dark grey flannel with a collar in white pique intended for wearing to job interviews and selected a skirt for Esme cut from a tweed suit sent in a parcel of good worn things by Bess, a sister of Mr McMahon who had promised temporary shelter for Sylvia in Sydney.

"I am sorry she cannot stay permanently," wrote Bess in reply to her brother's suggestion.

"But George and I have reached an agreement owing to all the relatives coming to stay with us since we came to Sydney." (George was a policeman.)

"I get no extra money from him when they are here and it is a struggle to keep the meals up.

"So we decided none of his come and none of mine.

"But Sylvia can stay until she gets a job and we will help her find a boarding place.

"Our Margaret is doing very well and got a raise last week. They are not putting any more girls on there."

Mrs McMahon got up from the machine now and laid Esme's skirl on the table to remove the pattern and put the pieces together for machining.

Sylvia stood too. Her mother did not appear to notice as she sat again and slipped the tweed under the machine needle. When the wheel began to whir Sylvia got up and let herself out of the kitchen.

The sky was right above her now with clouds idling across it in unconcerned fashion.

Her father and Frank and Lennie were finishing the day's farm jobs and Esme, Rose, Yvonne and Jackie were on the rails of the fence around the dairy watching. Esme was on the top rail her long thin legs dangling and Jackie who was three had his neck between the two lowest like one of the young calves.

"Sylly, Syllvy!" cried Esme seeing her.

Sylvia turned and made for the fence surrounding the house. She heard Jackie's wail and his cry "Take, me, take me!" and turned once as she scaled the fence to see his woeful moonlike face and the others sober too in the afternoon light.

She took a track that led to the well a slab covered hole of water of a milky substance that supplemented the tanks of rainwater during a dry spell and was used mostly for washing clothes and scrubbing the dairy.

Behind the well on a small rise there was a clump of wattles with roots raised above the ground forming

42

a kind of armchair. The spring that fed the well kept the grass there soft and green.

It was a place for Sylvia and the others to rest when they took the slide and cans to draw water.

If I am here in the winter I'll be carrying that blasted water again, she said to herself rocking her body and letting the roots hurt her.

The hills were folded in front of her to meet the sky and there was nothing much to gaze upon but tracks running through the grass even now threatening to turn a pale early winter brown.

Sylvia stood and grasped a branch of the wattle and shook it.

"I hate them! I hate them!" she cried.

Then she shut her eyes and laid her head on the branch until her anger was partly spent.

When she opened her eyes there was a horse and rider crossing the hill on one of the tracks.

"Arnold Wright!" she whispered, sinking down onto the grass. "I can see his buck teeth from here!"

Arnold was riding in the direction of the Wright farm one of the poorest in Berrigo. If she sat still and pulled a branch over her head he might not see her when he crossed the gully a little higher up riding by the straggling fence that divided the McMahons from their neighbour.

Seeing him with one eye a new thought struck Sylvia.

43

Berrigo would know she wasn't going to Sydney after all! She would have to face the Post Office crowd! She would drown herself first! She looked towards the well where the water winked between the slabs.

She saw herself pulled out by the armpits and all of them wailing while they watched.

She would look terrible with her hair plastered on her head and her clothes stuck to her body, perhaps her shoes missing. No she would not die that way.

She would walk to Sydney! Forgetting the proximity of Arnold Wright she pulled the branch aside to see where the road showed patches of beige coloured gravel through the trees. She could walk and walk and walk with the signposts telling her the way. She would leave at night when they were all asleep and would be too far away when they found her missing. She would arrive at Aunt Bess's and then it would be too late to be dragged home. The idea was so appealing she leapt to her feet and Arnold quite close now saw the flash of her old pink spotted dress. He jerked his surprised horse to a halt and after sitting a moment climbed down and tied the reins to a post. Sylvia was trapped. She could not run home and she could not escape Arnold striding towards her. She sank down onto the grass again.

"I thought it was you," Arnold said.

Who else would it be? Sylvia thought with scorn and snapped a twig off the wattle branch.

In the silence following she traced a pattern with it on the tree root.

"Gettin' in some practice for writin' home?" Arnold said squatting beside her.

Oh, what a clot! she thought, lifting her head.

But Arnold thought he had said something smart and stretched his lips farther over his teeth.

You think he's grinning all the time but he's not, Sylvia thought.

Arnold sobering drew his lips as far as they would reach to cover his teeth and glanced towards the road.

"I'd like to be goin'," he said.

"What would you do there?" said Sylvia half scornful although she had resolved not to speak to him just remain mute.

"Work. Get money," said Arnold.

Sylvia realized she had been pressing the twig deeply into the root when she heard it snap.

"See all that life," said Arnold. "Jeez, you're lucky."

Sylvia lifted her chin, shook back her hair and let the breath out of her body.

She was going! She was going!

She felt an overwhelming pity for Arnold. He was stuck on that terrible farm with a simpleton brother, hillbilly parents and grandmother and his young sister Nellie.

She looked into his face amazed that in spite of this fate he seemed normal, as normal as Arnold could be.

Does he think of drowning himself, she wondered.

Arnold looked at her leaning back wriggling her toes inside her old sandals.

"You'll miss the well chair," he said.

"How do you know we call it that?" she said.

"Esme told Nellie," he said.

He looked away and swallowed.

"I ask her," he said.

He gripped both his knees.

"About you," he said.

Sylvia felt her face warming.

The horse by the fence snorted and shook its head.

It startled them both.

"You should be going," Sylvia said.

He didn't move and she felt a small gladness that he didn't.

She stole a glance at his profile. Except for his teeth he wasn't bad looking. Arnold Wright good looking! She must be mad! She snorted not so loud as the horse and Arnold turned her way. He has nice eyes, she thought. Oh hell and damn! Those were the words she was going to use freely when she got to Sydney. She was going to paint her face and curl her hair, things she wasn't allowed at home. Oh God, if she didn't go! She moved her toes again curling them inside her sandals. Arnold saw. He looked as if he might lay a hand on her feet.

"Got chilblains?" he said.

Chilblains! Of all the impossible people Arnold was the most impossible! Daggy. That was the word for him. A word that was probably well aired in Sydney but not in Berrigo because it was too close to the bone.

Daggy sorts. Arnold was a daggy sort. She must get away! She had to go! She got to her feet as if she would take off then. Arnold was leaning on an elbow staring up at her.

She sat down again swiftly at the sound of steps. They were Esme's running along the track to the well.

Esme pulled up sharp when she saw them and stood legs apart several yards off as if reluctant to trespass upon their privacy.

"Come home, Mum says," she called.

Sylvia leaned back on an elbow slightly towards Arnold.

The spectacle caused Esme to stiffen like a small statue among the waving grass.

She plucked a piece and chewed it.

"Hullo Esme," called Arnold with something close to music in his voice.

It struck Sylvia that way too.

His voice should sound daggy, she said to herself glancing at him and deciding his teeth weren't so bad when he smiled a face splitting smile as he was doing now and showed them all.

"Mum's making gingerbread for our supper," Esme called.

Sylvia swallowed away the trickle of treacly syrup that invaded her saliva.

"She's making your blasted skirt!"

Arnold looked as if he liked her spirit.

Esme was astounded at the swear word.

"Oooooh, aaaah," she said both loud and hushed.

"Go home!" said Sylvia.

"She'll send me back!" said Esme.

"I won't be here," said Sylvia.

No one including Sylvia could work this out in that moment.

"I'm going for a ride on Arnold's horse!" Sylvia called out suddenly.

"You're not allowed," said Esme breaking a small silence involving them all even the horse who flung his ears back and his nose up.

"Can I?" said Sylvia turning to Arnold who would have gladly given her the horse along with himself.

She stood and he did a moment later.

"You ride behind," she said making for the fence.

Esme watched as Sylvia climbed the fence and slipped a leg across the saddle. The horse inquired with a shake of its neck. Arnold patted its rump soothingly then jumped on.

Sylvia took up the reins.

"Go home, pimp!" she called to Esme who after a moment started running hard towards the house.

Arnold wished there was no saddle to separate his body from Sylvia's. There was this hard raised rim under which he forced his crotch and Sylvia's beautifully rounded bottom at the end of her straight back seemed yards from him. He laid a hand just above her thigh. She didn't object so her laid the other hand near the other thigh.

Sylvia swished her head around and Arnold got a mouthful of her dark hair.

"Hang onto the saddle," Sylvia said.

Arnold obeyed. They moved off, the horse staying close by the fence and its rump broadening as they went up the incline.

When the fence turned a corner so did Sylvia and she kicked the horse into a canter down by the line of oaks on the western side of the McMahon's farm. Esme now on the woodheap by the house saw the flash of Sylvia's pink dress and raced inside to tell the others. When Sylvia and Arnold were clear of the oaks the McMahons like a small defending army were at the woodheap. The children not as tall as their parents stood on pieces of wood so they appeared a uniform group.

Sylvia pulled the horse up sharply and swung around to face them.

"Just what do you think you're up to, miss?" called Mrs McMahon across the couple of hundred yards separating them.

"Put your arms around me," said Sylvia low to Arnold.

Arnold placed his hands lightly at her waistline.

"Where they were before!" said Sylvia.

Arnold lowered them an inch.

Esme jumped from her block of wood to the ground and Mr McMahon took a few strides forward.

"Lovely goings on!" called Mrs McMahon.

"Them hands should be round cows' tits where they belong!" called Mr McMahon.

Arnold withdrew his hands and clung to the saddle.

"Put them back," said Sylvia low to Arnold.

Before he had time to Mrs McMahon called out again.

"There's no Sydney trip for you, miss!"

Esme gasped loud at this news and hopped in her agitation like a spider back onto the woodheap.

Arnold in deep shock looked for a change in Sylvia's expression.

She merely tilted her chin and lowered her lashes.

Under other circumstances Arnold might have crushed her small waist between his hands.

All he could do now was cling wretchedly to the saddle.

"Mum made the gingerbread!" called Esme.

"Shut up about the gingerbread!" said Mrs McMahon.

All of them heard the tears in her voice.

"Get down and come home!" said Mr McMahon somewhat feebly.

"I haven't finished my ride!" said Sylvia, pulling the horse's head back as if preparing to canter off.

"Getting around with Berrigo riff raff!" said Mrs McMahon.

"He's not riff raff!" called out Sylvia.

Arnold bowed his head longing to lay his forehead on Sylvia's neck.

Esme agitated at the thought of losing the friendship of Nellie when her mother's remark reached the Wright household gasped and hopped off the woodheap.

Mr McMahon took a couple more steps forward and picked up a stick lying in the grass, a piece from a quince tree abandoned by one of the children at play.

Who would he hit? thought Arnold. Please, not her!

Sylvia with her head up pulled the reins and the horse danced two or three little steps turning as it did, so that Sylvia and her father were almost face to face. Mr McMahon saw how her body flowed into the horse's body. They moved as one shape. She can ride, he thought, how well she can ride! Her hair swept past her cheek onto her neck. Her cheeks were pink from the ride and there was the rise of her bosom under the old spotted dress with the collar fastened loosely just above her breasts. If Arnold looked over her shoulder he could see between her breasts through the opening. Mr McMahon felt anger towards his wife. She had no right to sew clothes with openings in them like that!

Arnold sat in misery with his hands hanging on the horse's sides. Mr McMahon watched to see if his gaze fell over Sylvia's shoulders.

If he looks I'll kill him, Mr McMahon thought.

The buck toothed bastard, he's not getting her!

"Come home," he said hoping no one detected the pleading in his voice.

"There's nothing to go home for," Sylvia almost curled her lip towards the shabby old farmhouse with the smoking chimney.

Mr McMahon knew his wife would move a few steps towards him.

He saw her face creased and suddenly old.

"We've had enough of this, miss!" she called.

"Me too," said Sylvia.

"Listen to that cheek! It didn't take her long!" Mrs McMahon looked briefly and with hate at Arnold.

"Go on up inside," said Mr McMahon throwing a brief look at his wife.

"Huh!" she said ugly and angry. "Much good you've done! Haul her off that horse and send that riff raff packing!"

Arnold waited for Sylvia to say he wasn't riff raff.

But Sylvia's cool eyes held her father's eyes unwavering while the horse arched and swung its neck and took two more dancing steps.

"Use the stick on her!" shouted Mrs McMahon.

Mr McMahon looked at the stick as if he'd forgotten he held it.

Sylvia looked at it too and stretched her mouth in a little smile.

"Look at the cheeky grin!" cried Mrs McMahon.

It's not a cheeky grin, said the heart of Mr McMahon.

It's my daughter leaving me.

He threw the stick from him and turned and walked towards the house.

"Leaving me to do the dirty work!" shouted Mrs McMahon.

"Go to hell!" Mr McMahon shouted back.

She raced after him and caught him by his old blue shirt.

He pulled free and walked faster.

Mrs McMahon stood with her legs apart looking from him back to Sylvia and Arnold.

The wind whipped her apron like a white flag and Sylvia as if seeing it as a symbol of surrender climbed from the horse. She stood a moment with her face almost against the slippery leather of the saddle.

"I'll say goodbye," she whispered.

Arnold sat still with tears in his eyes. His mouth nearly covered his teeth as he hitched himself onto the saddle and when Sylvia turned away he slipped his feet into the stirrups and wheeled the horse around.

It allowed itself a shake of the head as if to say it knew all along things would finish this way.

Arnold did not turn his head when he cantered off.

Sylvia climbed the fence and Rose, Yvonne and Jackie ran to her and held her by the waist and legs. Esme and Lennie and Frank watched soberly from the woodheap.

Sylvia put Jackie on her back and made her way towards the house.

Mrs McMahon did too and near the woodheap stopped to pick up an armful of wood.

Sylvia stooped with Jackie still on her back and scraped up large chips dumping them in her skirt and gathering it up with one free hand.

"Lady Muck might soil her lily white hands!" cried Mrs McMahon.

"We'll do it!" said Esme.

They all went into the house.

Mr McMahon was sitting by the kitchen window with his hands on his knees.

He was looking out at the sky grey now.

Sylvia dropped the chips into the stove fire and put the kettle over the ring.

She sat and Jackie climbed on her knee and she linked her arms about him.

When the fire began to glow they showed smooth and white and round like the work of a sculptor.

Rose set the table and Esme sliced the gingerbread.

Mrs McMahon sat at the machine and let her face fall on her hand while she stared at the little pile of sewing.

Mr McMahon saw the white of the collar of Sylvia's dress now on the top of the pile.

He wanted to take it and tear it savagely between his hands.

But he sat with them still on his knees and said nothing.

Sylvia McMahon was away nearly two years before she was able to afford her train and coach fare home for a holiday.

She was seventeen and a half by this time.

Just as the family had talked of nothing else but her going away weeks ahead of the time, they seldom let drop the subject of her return.

"Let's mark every day off on the calendar!" cried Esme now twelve.

They all looked at the calendar, the one wall decoration in the kitchen.

Mrs McMahon turned her eyes back to the bowl of flour into which she was rubbing suet and turned the corners of her mouth down.

"Must you write all over everything?" she said, "Leave the calendar the way it is!"

"We would only make little marks!" said Esme.

"I said not to mark it at all!" said Mrs McMahon.

The pudding making went on and the children, Frank, Lennie, Esme, Rose, Yvonne and Jackie silently and unanimously agreed that the subject of Sylvia's homecoming should be dropped for the moment.

"Mum's sort of cranky about Sylly coming home," Rose said to Esme when they were outside.

They were ordered by their mother to go to the cream box at the roadside and collect groceries left there by the general carrier for Berrigo.

It was cold walking in the wind and the girls pulled a slide between them to carry the things home.

Esme with her head down said sharply: "Don't call her Sylly!"

Rose in awe of Esme as Esme was in awe of Sylvia couldn't find words to say the pet name meant loving Sylvia.

Esme took a pace or two ahead of Rose to express disapproval and Rose panted to keep up.

"We could draw a little calendar and keep it in our pants drawer," panted Rose to the back of Esme's neck.

It looked in disagreement.

No calendar was drawn and hidden but the days passed just the same.

Finally Sylvia came.

"We'll all go to the Post Office to meet her!" Esme cried.

The coach from the nearest rail head brought passengers to the Berrigo Post Office.

Mrs McMahon was stuffing wood into the stove when Esme spoke.

She straightened and slammed the stove door shut.

"That would be stupid!"

Esme braver now that Sylvia was nearly here answered with spirit.

"That way we can all be with her for the longest possible time!"

"Two weeks and she'll be gone again!" said Mrs McMahon.

Briefly the eyes of all the children accused her as she went with her strutting step to the dresser to take out a mixing bowl.

She broke eggs into it and the children thought there could have been a better pudding offered for Sylvia's return than baked custard.

"Who would stay here to keep the fire going and start the milking if we all charged off to hang around like the rest of Berrigo?" said Mrs McMahon.

She scorned the practice of waiting on the mail every day at the Post Office. She seldom went into town at all due mainly to the family's almost constant state of debt. When the general store bill was paid there would be a few pounds hanging onto the butcher's bill from earlier lean months or the baker could only be paid at the end of alternate months.

Not only was Mrs McMahon afraid of coming face to face with her creditors but she felt the eyes of all Berrigo were on her accusing her of these shortcomings.

In the end it was Lennie, Esme and those younger who went to meet Sylvia. Frank at sixteen was nearly a man and not to be spared to any leisurely caper like meeting a coach.

Esme was downcast. She was an avid reader and characters in books spent a lot of time in loving communication. Fathers embraced mothers and parents openly kissed and hugged their children.

She fell a little behind the others dreaming of the McMahons carrying on this way. She imagined them spread across the road arm in arm joyful in their anticipation of meeting Sylvia. When Esme lifted her head to face reality they had rounded the last bend and Berrigo, the coach and Sylvia came into view.

"It's there!" screamed Rose and Lennie flung Jackie on his back and the five of them raced the few hundred yards pulling up and moving into a bunch when they had almost reached Sylvia.

She stood holding her case taller than they remembered her wearing a dress they had never seen.

"Sylly, Sylly!" cried Esme forgetting.

Rose gasped a reminder.

Lennie plunged forward to take her case the old one she went away with.

"Something terrible happened just before I left," said Sylvia looking back over her shoulder to see who of Berrigo was staring from the Post Office.

Oh, what what?

Sylvia with five pairs of eyes fixed on her wet her lips which her sisters observed were outlined in lipstick and flashed her eyes away from them.

"I got a new one and had it packed to bring and left it behind.

"I left it sitting on the table of the flat. I must have."

Oh, poor Sylvia.

"It had presents in it too."

The sympathy of the children was transferred immediately to themselves.

Presents! What could they have been?

"What were they!" said Lennie.

"It doesn't matter!" Esme cried. "Poor Syll—Sylvia!"

"I'm not called that now," said Sylvia walking rapidly and stretching the legs of Jackie to their limit.

"What is your name then?" said Lennie with the smallest edge of scorn to his voice.

Esme shot a look of warning at him.

"Is it Maud?" said Rose with reference to Sylvia's second name.

Esme looked fearfully into Sylvia's face before throwing Rose a withering look.

"Sylvarnia most of the time," said Sylvia as if she hadn't heard. "Varnia sometimes for short."

She was walking fast with her chin up and lowered eyes and the others were fully taxed trying to keep up with her and read her expression.

Lennie dropped the case suddenly in the middle of the road and stood legs apart. The others halted and Sylvia too slowed a little.

Lennie blew out his cheeks and looked as if he might say something. Esme pleaded with her eyes not to. But Lennie had lowered his to look at the case and fix his gaze on the label attached to the handle. He turned it towards him and putting his head slightly to one side read it silently. It said "Miss Sylvia McMahon, Passenger to Berrigo".

Lennie picked up the case almost with a smile on his face and walked with new energy. Esme raced to Sylvia and took her hand.

"We should have a car to come and meet you," she whispered for none of the others to hear.

"I thought Father might have bought one," said Sylvia.

Father. That was a new way of addressing him who had been Dad as long as Esme could remember.

She looked anxiously back but the others had not heard. They marched in a little army with Lennie bent sideways by the case.

Esme saw with surprise they had reached the big gate to the farm with the cream box on the roadside. She looked into Sylvia's face for signs that she might have remembered collecting bread and groceries there, crushed inside to shelter from rain, or sitting with dangling legs for a rare visitor who might otherwise miss turning in. But there was nothing to read on Sylvia's thick white skin, bluish lidded eyes and folded red mouth.

There was not much of a walk now to the house, a few dozen yards with saplings and dog bush obscuring the view, then into the clear and there it was inside its crooked fence, small and grey like a crouched mouse.

There were only two real bedrooms. The other for Frank and Lennie was a closed-off end of the verandah that did not keep out the weather and when there was a big storm the boys, bedding and all, were moved into the sitting room to finish their sleep among the table, chairs and chiffonier legs.

The girls and Jackie had the second bedroom and the thought hit Esme now that Sylvia would not take too kindly to making a fifth in the already overcrowded space.

"You'll be having my bed and Mum'll make a bed for Vonnie on the couch," Esme said but the whisper was clearly heard by Yvonne whose seven year old face creased with anger.

"You keep slipping off!" she said.

"I'll sleep with Rose and Jackie and you can have the bed to yourself," Esme said ignoring the outburst.

The thought of someone with a bed to themselves sobered and silenced the McMahons and they held onto this small miracle while they trudged a few more steps.

But it did not stay with Yvonne too long.

"You're making all that up!" she cried.

Esme was about to shout a denial when they saw Mrs McMahon had come onto the verandah her two hands on the rail.

"She's come!" cried Esme unnecessarily.

Soon there was nothing but a narrow flower bed between Mrs McMahon and Sylvia.

In books, thought Esme, Mrs McMahon would have leaned over and clutched Sylvia and the flowers would have been trampled uncaringly in the embrace.

"Come round," said Mrs McMahon, "Don't tread on the bulbs."

When they were bunched together and Mrs McMahon close enough to touch Sylvia, Mr McMahon and Frank in their old milking clothes stepped up onto the verandah from the other end.

Frank was carrying a bucket with the house milk in it and he held it out as if to say this was the real reason for coming.

"Put that milk on the kitchen table with a cover over it," said Mrs McMahon.

"Look at her, Dad!" cried Esme.

Mr McMahon was looking. His eyes were level with the top of her head and hers with his chin. His chin and her chin had the same cleft. Their eyes though not quite meeting were washed with the same toffee brown liquid. Each mouth quirked slightly with the same shy smile.

Mrs McMahon stepped between them like a bustling hen leading chickens to somewhere else.

"There's things for all of you to do!" cried Mrs McMahon taking her apron from a chair and pinning it rapidly on.

The children lingered somewhat dreamily some of them leaning against chairs as if they thought it more appropriate to sit but Mrs McMahon pushed the chairs under the table and the guilty ones had to move fast to avoid being pinned there too.

"The place for that's in the bedroom," said Mrs McMahon of Sylvia's case and Lennie having just dropped it thankfully picked it up again.

Mr McMahon suddenly looking as if he wanted to get his face out of the way hurried off with Frank following.

The kitchen had emptied of all of them except Sylvia, Esme, Rose and Yvonne.

"Sit on a chair," said Esme to Sylvia.

Sylvia sat and took off her little round black hat and held it on her knees.

They saw her fluffed-out black hair with the deep wave running right round it.

"Let me do it!" cried Esme her hands hovering over Sylvia's head as if they already held brush and comb.

"We've got to set the table!" said Rose.

Sylvia tilted her face and shook her thick, beautiful bouncy hair.

"I'm having it waved when I get back. Little waves all around my face."

She drew with her two forefingers a scalloped edge to her cheeks.

"Oh, oh!" cried Esme looking to Rose and Yvonne to say with her eyes how splendid this would be.

But Rose and Yvonne setting the table frowned at the knives and forks.

"We'll tell Mum you didn't help!"

"You pair of pimps!" said Esme nearly leaning against Sylvia.

"Nellie Wright might be over to play tomorrow," said Rose with lowered eyes and significant cunning.

"She wouldn't like Arnold now!" cried Esme.

Sylvia's face said nothing and her long fine fingers stroked the crown of her hat.

"I'm dying to see all your things," whispered Esme.

"I didn't bring everything," said Sylvia. "They would've been crushed up in the case."

To have dresses and hats to leave behind! Even Rose and Yvonne finishing the table setting lifted their heads at this.

"I'm sitting next to you at supper," whispered Esme turning her eyes towards Rose and Yvonne daring them to dispute this.

They each made a half toss of their heads putting the sugar bowl and milk jug each with a beaded cover and the jam and butter with great care in the centre of the table.

Esme did sit next to Sylvia at supper but she would have been better next to Lennie.

"Ask Varnia to pass the bread," he whispered in an aside to Yvonne which Esme heard.

She reached past Rose and Yvonne and pulled at the shirt on Lennie's shoulder twisting it about.

Fighting at the meal table, even talking to excess was not tolerated by either parent and Mr McMahon slapped the bread knife so sharply on the table some of the things rattled about.

Esme with swift eyes towards Sylvia noticed how fussily with her lovely slender hands she put her bread and butter plate back in its place and straightened the pudding spoon which had gone askew. Esme immediately made similar adjustments at her place.

"Look at her," whispered Rose to Yvonne.

"You've asked God's blessing on this food. Don't make a mockery of it!" said Mrs McMahon and although she didn't look Sylvia's way Esme felt Mrs McMahon was laying the blame on her.

Esme sneaked a hand down to touch the cool waistline of Sylvia's dress.

Sylvia brushed some breadcrumbs on the tablecloth into a little heap and dropped them onto her plate and laid the knife at a perfect angle across it.

Esme wanted to but daren't do the same at her place.

After supper they did the usual things like washing up and Mr McMahon, Frank and Lennie went out in the half dark for more wood, to see that the dairy was locked against dogs and fowls and that calves in their paddock had no chance of joining mothers and sucking them dry by morning.

Esme would have liked her father to have suggested they all go to the sitting room and light a fire there and let Sylvia entertain them with stories of her life in the city.

Esme pictured Sylvia at the table with its ruby red cloth stroking it with her fine white fingers and the lamplight making a cameo of her face with her hair lost in the shadows.

Perhaps she would change her dress for them. People in books changed their clothes a lot particularly in the evening. The best that could be expected of the McMahons was for Mrs McMahon to take her apron off and Mr McMahon to discard his blucher boots for an old pair of patent leather shoes he danced in during the early days of their marriage. The children under a rigid rule changed into old things no longer worth mending as soon as they came in from school or church.

But Esme thought it was best to leave the idea of a family gathering a dream.

Mrs McMahon's face had tightened more than once at supper when Esme talked about her job and flat in Sydney. Esme thought her mother rose unnecessarily and sharply a couple of times to put the teapot back on the stove bringing about a break in the talk.

At bedtime Esme and even Rose and Yvonne were disappointed that Sylvia shook from her case the night-dress her mother made her to go away.

"You can see right through my new ones," Sylvia said.

Oh.

Mrs McMahon came in with the lamp and blew out their candle. She wasn't making up a bed on the couch for anyone but taking Jackie to share the double bed with his parents.

Esme raised herself in bed.

"She's wearing the nightie you made her," she said.

Mrs McMahon raised the lamp.

"It's ironed up very nice," she said.

"A woman at the flats did it for me," Sylvia said, "She brings in my clothes from the line and irons them all and puts them outside my door.

"She would do anything in the world for me."

Mrs McMahon turned to leave.

"Don't talk but get right to sleep or your father'll be in with the strap."

Esme crushed her cheek on Sylvia's shoulder hating her mother.

"Not you," she whispered.

She laid an arm across Sylvia's waist.

"We can whisper," she said. "They won't hear."

Light from the window outlined Sylvia's features and her spread hair.

"Tell me all about your little flat," Esme whispered.

"It's not little. The sitting room is as big as all this house."

Mindful of the rule about not talking Esme's gasp went inward.

"As big as this house except for the kitchen," Sylvia amended.

"And where you work?" Esme whispered.

"It's big too. Everyone has their own desk. I have the best."

"How do you know what to do?" whispered Esme and the heads of Rose and Yvonne rose like fish from a lake.

"I know. I show the new girls when they come."

She lifted her hands from the bedclothes and held them up to catch the light and arranged them as if they were to be painted.

"You typewrite, don't you?" whispered Esme.

"I'm fast too," said Sylvia.

"Are there boys?" whispered Esme.

"Men!" said Sylvia too loud and the larger bedroom heard.

"I warned you!" called out Mrs McMahon and Mr McMahon winced.

"It's natural she'd talk," he said.

"Skite!" said Mrs McMahon. She wriggled her body so that Jackie fitted into the curve between stomach and thighs.

Mr McMahon wriggled too.

"Put him on the other side of you," he whispered.

"They'd hear," said Mrs McMahon.

Through the wall Esme put her lips close to Sylvia's ear.

"Do they want you to you-know-what?" she whispered.

"Of course," said Sylvia.

Esme drew back to study Sylvia's lovely remote profile.

"You don't?" she said.

Sylvia was silent.

So was Mr McMahon with his profile also outlined by the moonlight.

Across Jackie Mrs McMahon saw.

His lips tucked in at the corners were finely sculptured like Sylvia's.

She rose slightly in bed but he did not turn his head. Angry she pulled at her pillow.

"I'll get her working tomorrow!" she said. "Sitting about with her hands in her lap! Lady Muck! She'll work the same as the others do!"

"She'll probably do it well too," said Mr McMahon.

Very still he felt he was about to leave his warm bed and step into the icy flooded current of Berrigo Creek.

"She's a housemaid."

"A what?" shrieked Mrs McMahon and to quieten her he put a hand across Jackie and laid it on her thigh. He felt it quiver like the flesh of a young horse he was breaking in.

"She's got an office job!" said Mrs McMahon.

"She couldn't get one. Bess wrote and told us."

"Us? Why don't I know?"

"Bess wrote when she left there and said it was a good place. It's not to say she won't get an office job when times get better."

"Bess pushed her out! She was frightened she might get something better than their Margaret. I know that one! She'd be glad she's only a maid!"

Only a maid, thought Mrs McMahon her flesh no longer quivering.

I was a maid.

"You were a maid," said Mr McMahon, "You were all right."

71

Mrs McMahon for a moment wanted to steer his hand towards her inner thigh. But she raised her knees and it slid away to lie indifferently on Jackie's stomach.

"You knew all that time and you didn't say! I see where she gets her lies and deceit from!"

"Bess wrote and I got the letter in the mail one day when I picked it up. Just by chance." Mr McMahon a fairly devout Catholic appeared still grateful to God for organizing this.

"All that blowing and skiting and her a maid! No more than a housemaid.

"I'll bowl her out!" cried Mrs McMahon. "First chance I get and there'll be plenty I'll bowl her out!

"I'll bowl her out with pleasure!" cried Mrs McMahon when Mr McMahon did not speak.

He turned his face and looked at her only for a moment before turning back and with his shoulders shutting her away.

Mrs McMahon resisted an impulse to grasp his shoulder and turn him towards her.

She was raised enough in the bed to see only the tip of his ear and his black hair swirling around the crown of his head.

Look at me, she cried inside her and the tears got into her voice.

"Deceiving me like that!"

Mr McMahon turned then and she fell back onto the pillow.

"Lift Jackie to the other side," he whispered.

Afterwards they put Jackie back and he was folded warm and moist against the warm and moist body of Mrs McMahon.

Mr McMahon raised himself on his elbows.

"Don't bowl her out straight away," he said. "Leave it just for a day or two."

Sleep was coming to Mrs McMahon gently like a soft blanket pulled across her brain.

Only a maid, she thought. A housemaid.

No better than me after all.

She opened the refrigerator door and said to the inside of it: "We should visit them."

Turning around with the milk she looked at the back of his neck as if it would answer her.

She thought it drooped with eyes down.

She took her place at the table not looking into his face but pulling her scrambled eggs to her.

When the kettle boiled she turned to the stove to attend to it and it was his turn to study the back of her neck.

Her thick hair was combed upwards into a bun but a few strands escaped and trailed onto her collar without taking anything from her air of neatness.

He saw her shoulders move when she poured water into the teapot and glimpsed her profile.

How strong she is, he thought. I wish I were strong like her.

When she was sitting down again he said: "Couldn't we ask them to come here?"

He looked around the kitchen which she seemed always to be adding to. One corner was filled with a string of baskets starting near the ceiling. They were like big straw pockets filled with her recipe books, tea towels and the bottom two with vegetables. Dried ferns sprouted uselessly from an old pottery jug which had the cracked part turned to the wall, and she had painted over an old-fashioned washing board, her latest find, and hung it to use as a notice board on which she pinned messages to herself or him, recipes and household hints.

Perhaps this sort of thing wasn't their taste. No, it was better to see their place first.

Her face tightened.

"You don't do it that way," she said not as mildly as she usually did when he made similar blunders.

Yet it was he who had gone to a good boarding school and then to University to take a science degree, and she who had left State school at sixteen and become a typist.

She was working in the city headquarters of the Forestry Commission when she met him.

Six months ago the Commission appointed him to work from a small office in this small timber town providing a cottage on the outskirts, the first you came upon to suggest the huddle of cottages and shops half a mile on.

She liked the place the minute she saw it, particularly the view of the hills and the sweep of pine forests which never seemed to excite the locals who owned or worked in the two general stores, the bakery, butcher's, two banks, newsagents, post office, two timber mills or had small dairy farms or larger cattle runs.

The school and schoolhouse were at the other end of the town, set apart like the forestry cottage perhaps to suggest transients were people a little apart from the locals.

There were churches but no resident ministers.

Louisa did her shopping quickly and efficiently and came back to sit with her crochet—she had made their bedspread and was at work on one for the spare room—looking at the hills where the clouds sometimes gathered above a tall peak.

"Like a bride taking off her wedding veil," she said once to herself.

She wrote a lot of long letters, the replies brought home by her husband because all their mail went to the Forestry office in the absence of a mailman.

She rebuilt the garden keeping one of the tanks for garden water and buying potted cuttings from the street stalls that seemed to be held every other Friday by one or another of the numerous local charities.

"You should join in with us," said one of the stall-holders once glancing at her middle flat under her camel coloured skirt.

"When she settles down," said the other stallholder whose eyes were kind in her ruddy farmer's face.

It was Jim who learned that his former fiancée had come to live in or rather near the little town.

"You wouldn't guess who I saw today," he said coming into the kitchen one evening where the smell of quinces lingered. She had lined up her jars of pale pink jelly on a bench top so full of pleasure in her handiwork she could not bear to put them away in a cupboard just yet.

She waited for him to tell her.

"Annie," he said.

"Really?" she said.

He went into the bedroom to hang up his coat and she waited for him to come back.

"Passing through?" she said as he went by into the scullery off the kitchen which they used to wash their hands because the old-fashioned bathroom was off the back verandah.

She liked it though after the city home she was reared in with a white tiled sterile bathroom and toilet near the bedrooms.

"No," he said taking his place at the table. "She's living here."

"Married?" she said.

"They bought the farm Craggy Hills had for sale," he said by way of saying she was, and slipping easily into local jargon in a way she had not yet acquired.

He ate some of his dinner before he told her more.

"It was funny," he said. "But I was driving past the farm a week ago and I started to think about her. I'd just glimpsed these two going up the drive from the front gate. They had their backs to me and I started to think about her. I must have recognized her unconsciously."

"Yes, you must have," she said dryly.

If the subject had been a different one he might have laughed his there-I-go-again laugh but this time he picked up a piece of bread she had taken to making lately. His face had reddened.

"How was your day?" he said after a while.

"OK. A Mrs Henning or Hanning rang and asked for something for a church street stall. How do they know I'm C of E?"

"They know everything," he said.

She took one of her jars of quince jelly—after a couple of days she could bear to part with it—and a crochet cushion cover and was delivering them to the stall and receiving effusive thanks when she saw a woman she knew to be Annie coming out of the bakery.

She was smallish, slim and quick and she got into a truck and drove off.

A week later Louisa was shopping late on a Friday—the little town kept a custom from early days of its settlement and stayed open till eight o'clock on Friday evening—and went to Jim's office to go home with him.

Annie and a man, her husband obviously, were standing under the roof that extended over the footpath outside the office. Jim had his back to them locking the door. Louisa was on the other side and they unconsciously made a foursome.

Jim came down the two steps.

"Hullo, Annie," he said.

She raised a small face framed with fair hair under a woollen cap. The evening was grey with a mist of rain.

"Peter my husband," Annie said. "Jim Taylor."

My God, he's not going to introduce me, Louisa thought.

It was Peter who smiled at her. "Mrs Taylor," he said "Annie, my wife."

"Louisa," Jim murmured almost as an afterthought.

There was a silence only as long as an intake of breath.

"We could go for a drink," Peter said inclining his head towards the hotel next door but one from the Forestry office.

"Peter, the baby!" Annie cried almost scandalized.

"Yes, yes! I forgot," he said.

Forget the baby? said the quick frown on Annie's face.

79

"Bye, bye," they said together and made for their truck and obviously their baby.

Louisa saw Annie the following week on the other side of the street in the town. Louisa stood still with her parcels and smiled and Annie hesitated at the door of the truck. A big timber lorry rumbled slowly between them and when it passed Annie was backing the truck her chin lifted and her eyes on the rear window.

Louisa walked the half mile to her house glad to see its friendly winking windows and surprised she got there so quickly.

She filled in the afternoon weeding the earth around her tomatoes, rubbing vaseline into her summer shoes and putting them away in tissue paper and reading for a while in the sun on the front verandah wondering through her distraction why she felt a vague depression and seeing from time to time the lift of Annie's chin as she backed the truck.

"I must learn to drive," Louisa said aloud as she often did when alone.

It was a couple of days after that during breakfast she said they should go and visit Annie and Peter.

"What is their name?" she said.

"Pomfrey," he said and she wondered briefly how he found out.

"Did you know him at all?" Louisa asked.

"No," he said.

"Well, we should go and visit them," she said.

"Do you read all these things in books?" he said.

"People know by instinct what to do," she said and felt she almost disliked him.

"We were here first and they have come and don't know anyone," she said after a little silence.

"We call on them and take something."

Her eyes strayed to her kitchen shelves lined with bottles of preserves, deciding whether to take her peaches which were the more successful or her apricots which she could have cooked a little longer.

She put the apricots with four tomatoes in varying shades of ripeness into a basket the next afternoon which was a Saturday. Then she added a loaf of her bread changing it for a larger one, and then a smaller one and finally going back to the one she chose first.

He glanced into the basket when he came into the kitchen in a pullover she had knitted him.

"This all right?" he said indicating his pullover and pants.

"This all right?" she said half humourously indicating the basket.

"You would know," he said.

When they were nearly there he said: "They mightn't be home," but she couldn't tell from his profile whether he hoped they wouldn't be.

They were. Standing on their steps they appeared to be deciding what they could do with the front garden neglected for years by Craggy Hills.

81

"This is really nice of you," Peter said coming down to meet them.

He tipped the basket to show Annie as if urging her to enthusiasm.

Annie had a nice wide smile that transformed her small face.

Louisa felt her own face was too big, in spite of the thick fringe she wore to shorten it.

"Come on in, come on in," said Peter.

He is doing all the hosting, Louisa thought. We'll leave very soon.

But they stayed and ate dinner with them.

Annie put the apricots out in a dish and Louisa wished she had brought the peaches.

"We like them chewy," Louisa said. "I hope you do too."

"They'll be lovely," Annie said. "We mean to grow fruit."

She glanced through the funny little window to see Peter and Jim making their way back after an hour's absence.

"Here they come," Louisa said with relief.

The two pairs of eyes watched them.

"One saves the trees and the other cuts them down," Louisa said laughingly.

Annie wasn't amused. "Peter won't cut anything down that should be saved," she said going to pick up the baby and taking him to the window to see his father.

"See Daddy coming?" she said making Louisa feel even more foolish because she was a stranger to babies.

She thought the child unattractive with large very red cheeks. It amazed her further that the parents considered this a redeeming feature and pointed them out in case Louisa and Jim didn't notice which appeared an impossibility.

Even now Annie couldn't resist plucking one of the cheeks.

"Old Poppy Cheeks," she said.

Oh God, we're going to be here for hours yet, Louisa thought gazing at the table.

The men came in. Louisa looked up expecting an apology but their faces wore a sort of self congratulatory look for leaving the women together.

"This is nice," said Peter seeing the table set.

They ate some canned soup, a salad with ham from a tin and the apricots with cream.

My bread is the best part of the meal, Louisa thought and began to plan a menu to serve them when the visit was returned.

I'll show her, she thought watching Peter eat the uninspiring salad with obvious relish.

They were more than half way home before they spoke. He is waiting for me to say something about them (her) she thought.

Out of habit because it was always she who started a conversation no matter what the occasion, she fished around in her mind for something to say.

Then she thought: By hell, I won't mention them! I won't say anything at all about them!

She glanced out of the car window passing a cottage near the road with a side wall thickly crusted with a kind of ivy studded with small creamy flowers.

"See that!" she said and he jerked with the suddeness of her speech.

"It's gone now, but it was a climbing plant. I'll get some slips of it from somewhere and plant it by the garage to cover that ugly side near the house."

He drove a way before answering.

"You're the gardener," he said.

It became easier and easier as the evening ended not to talk about the visit or Annie and Peter.

"Do you want coffee?" she said when she was in her dressing gown and he had finished listening to a news commentary on the radio.

To herself she said: "It will be better than the stuff they gave us."

She made the coffee as she usually did stirring a little cream in at the end and dusting it lightly with cinnamon.

"Soon be time to light a fire," she said. "I'm dying to try out the fireplace."

They have one too, she thought and saw in her mind the child sitting looking at it from the floor with its big red cheeks getting redder.

I wonder what he thought of the baby, she thought.

She stood up sharply and rinsed her cup at the sink.

"Do you have anything planned for tomorrow?" she asked.

In the silence before he answered she wondered if a free agent that he was in his job he would drop in on them without mentioning it.

Before she fell asleep she thought: The whole night passed without a word about them. Remarkable.

Even more remarkable was the weeks that passed after that without a word about them.

By then Louisa had put them quite a distance from her mind and ceased to look out for the truck when shopping in the town.

On a sunny, windy Wednesday she went off to post four letters she had written that morning.

They were long owed and she had written at length with some of her phrases still going round and round in her mind. *Frosts are beginning to breathe on us*, she wrote to her Aunt Cissie. *Little knife blades are coming up in the lawn. I can't wait to see what prize will be spiked on the end.*

Aunt Cissie would enjoy that. Louisa saw her showing the letter around and saying that Louisa had a way with words. "It's her way of describing her bulbs coming out." Aunt Cissie would say.

Louisa in her oldish overcoat with the belt swinging ran up the Post Office steps and stopped dead when she came face to face with Annie standing near the post boxes.

Annie in a peaked tweed cap, thick sweater and nicely cut brown trousers had a large manila envelope in one hand and her child held on her hip by the other.

Louisa saw the address on the envelope. The Department of External Studies, University of —. The baby's leg covered the remainder but Louisa guessed it to be the University west of the range about two hundred miles off.

Something for him, she thought. No, it was a feminine hand, almost certainly Annie's.

"Hullo, Poppy Cheeks," she said to the baby. Annie looked pleased, the baby moved its leg and Louisa got another look at the envelope.

The address of the sender in the top corner was Mrs Annie Pomfrey.

She was at University when she was engaged to Jim, Louisa remembered. She left when they broke it off. Now she is studying again.

Both women continued to look at the baby as if he were the only subject they had in common.

"He loves an outing," Annie said.

The baby jigged as if in agreement and Annie laughed with pride as if here was further proof of his brightness.

"We must have you over," Louisa said after a moment realizing it must be said.

"Thank you," Annie said, hitching the child perhaps to say he was heavy and she wasn't going to stay there too long.

She turned to slip her letter into the post box and Louisa went into the office to buy her stamps.

I should have said goodbye or something, Louisa worried when the porch was empty of the two of them on her way out.

Even the truck was gone from the main street and Louisa felt a strange rejection as if Annie had cut short her stay in the town to be rid of her.

She fought an urge that night at dinner to bring up the subject of the Pomfreys.

I have held out this long why spoil it now, she thought wondering what there was to spoil.

She watched Jim eating his dessert noticing when his spoon cut deep into it how perfect was the layer of cake, jam, more cake and custard topping.

"Very nice indeed," he said when he put his plate aside.

Pleased she got up and made up a plateful of cheese and crackers.

He went ahead of her into the living room and she carried in the coffee and set the tray on a table between their two big chairs. A lamp was on and the room looked homely and intimate with floorboards polished to a high shine under her scatter rugs, pottery jugs filled with berries and dried leaves, several small tables, the old-fashioned chiffonier and pictures grouped on the walls. Nothing expensive but tasteful and with an invitation to relax. She did, sipping her coffee and running her eyes over her possessions, resting them on the bookcase with books tightly packed on the shelves. Two were out, sitting on the cabinet below the shelves. Did she not put them back when she was dusting?

She stared obeying an impulse not to get up. After a while she could read the titles. A volume of Sheridan's plays and *The History of Greece*. A feeling washed over her. She looked at him but he was innocently reading the newspaper, a morning one printed in Sydney but not reaching the little town until later afternoon.

He folded a part he had read and put it aside.

"I read the paper more thoroughly now I don't see it till night," he said.

She did not speak.

"I've finished with the news part," he said.

She finished her coffee and went to the kitchen.

He is happier now, happier than he was before she thought looking around the kitchen trying to draw comfort from it but it seemed to recede from her. She filled the sink with hot water to wash up.

"Like some help?" he called out as he usually did.

"I'm OK," she said, keeping her answer as brief as possible.

She always washed the dinner set herself, not trusting anyone else to handle the treasured pieces.

She got into her nightwear soon after that and only went once into the living room to collect his coffee cup and the tray.

"An early night?" he said seeing her in her gown over the edge of his paper.

He's become quite talkative, she thought in bed with the paper not so much to read but to coax on sleep.

The books were still there next morning after he had gone to work.

Just before he was due home for dinner she put them back, closing the glass doors and rubbing her duster around the wood.

She stared at the lock thinking of taking the key away, aware that she was not the kind of person to lose keys.

"Don't be foolish," she said going into the kitchen.

The books stayed in their place the next day and the day after that.

After the weekend they were still there.

I must suggest going somewhere for a weekend or joining a group she told herself as if she were fighting some sort of nervous disorder.

A few days later she was in the kitchen wiping out the refrigerator when Peter appeared in the doorway in his farmer's overalls clasping a large pumpkin to his stomach.

"Goodness! Hullo!" she said opening the screen door to let him in.

The pumpkin wobbled to stillness on the kitchen table.

"For me?" she said "All of that?"

Without being asked he sat on the edge of one of the kitchen chairs with their tied-on frilled red check cushions.

She laid a hand on the grey-blue skin of the pumpkin as she might have touched a beautiful fur wrap.

"Pumpkin pie, pumpkin soup, pumpkin scones! And I'll preserve some," she said.

"Bottled pumpkin?" he said looking at her shelves of preserves.

She took a knife from a drawer and when she went to cut it he got up and took the knife from her and slapped it through the skin cracking the pumpkin open as if it were some great nut.

The flesh was a deep rich orange running to meet the skin.

Wordlessly they stood admiring.

"Cut a wedge," she said indicating where.

He did swiftly and cleanly and she took the piece to the sink.

"I'll make some scones now," she said.

While she peeled the pumpkin she half-turned to continue talking to him.

She switched on the small electric cooker which she used only in emergencies, cooking most of the time on the wood stove.

"This is an emergency," she said to herself.

"This is nice," he said lifting his head and looking around the kitchen.

She thought of their place, the toys on the living room floor, the end of the dining room table cluttered and the bench near the sink piled with dishes, washed and unwashed. Wherever you looked there seemed to be the child's clothes.

She put the lid on the saucepan and wiped her hands.

"Come and see the rest of it," she said.

"Oh, my," he said looking with admiration around the living room standing in the doorway. When she turned and went into the bedroom he followed.

The bed was one she had bought at an auction sale of dark wood she had polished to a soft, warm lustre. He went to it and put a hand in some carving at the foot, smoothing the edges and glancing at the matching inlet on the other side.

"Perfect," he said, "Perfect."

He looked around at the dressing table with her things laid on it and past the high wardrobe to a small window near the ceiling.

He stared long at the frilled white curtains and she did not think it necessary to tell him she had made them.

"I threw out the old linoleum," she said tapping the floor with her shoe. She had stained the boards and laid a beige-coloured rug near the bed.

Going out and crossing the front verandah he followed her.

She told him what she planned to do with the garden which ran steeply to the road. How she would plant ferns and vines and flowering cactus for colour in the summer and to hold the earth from slipping to the roadway.

"I'll work it all round these rocks," she said, walking with him over them, emerging now from a mass of uncontrolled growth. As she spoke she bent and pulled at some grass ripping it away to show more rock. He bent and pulled it with her and she straightened holding the long loop of root against her skirt as if it were a bridal bouquet.

They looked down on the truck, its nose pointing to the town.

He started to move to the path leading to the road, head down and hands in his overall pockets.

Come in for a scone on your way home, she called silently to the back of his neck.

He turned his face.

"I'll call in on my way back for one of those scones," he said.

She ran up to the house.

Oh lovely verandah, lovely old chair she said to herself passing them and hearing the tiny bubbling sound of the pumpkin cooking.

I really need to see more people, she thought tipping flour into a bowl. I'll ask him for some suggestions.

What did he do before the farming? she thought, seeing his hands again. That little scar near his ear. How did he get it? Oh, stop it, stop it, she said to herself slapping the dough harder than she should.

He did not call in on his way home.

She turned the scones from their tray and threw a tea towel over them and went and sat with her book on the verandah surreptitiously to watch for him.

When she went to the mirror later in the afternoon to do her hair she saw her sad eyes and her vacant face.

"Oh, this blasted long face!" she said as if it were to blame and snatching the brush to fluff up her fringe.

Next day he telephoned. She thought about such an event but never expected it knowing them to be still waiting for a phone to be connected.

He rang from the telephone booth at the Post Office.

"I didn't call in," he said.

"You were short on time," she said knowing by the silence following this was not true.

"How were the scones?" he said.

"Nice and light, a good colour."

She heard the noise of a big truck rumbling through the town.

"I rang to say sorry I didn't call," he said.

"That's OK," she said, "Goodbye."

93

She ran to the mirror and looked at her face.

"It's not too long after all," she said, brushing the pieces of hair she had trained over her ears and turning her face to admire her jawline.

She lowered her eyes and tipped back her head the way Annie had done in the truck that day.

She darted out of the room smiling.

Next evening carrying the tray of coffee into the living room the books were out sitting on the cabinet again.

She stared at them standing by the table and Jim lifted his eyes from his paper to follow her gaze.

"Those books," she said, "I thought I put them back on the shelves."

He slapped his paper, not too hard.

"You're too damn fussy," he said. "A couple of books out of a shelf!"

She sat and took up her coffee.

She sipped it, seeing Peter in the doorway looking with loving eyes on the room.

"Some people like order," she said. "I for one."

Him too, she thought laying the china cup on its saucer wondering if he would like the shape and pattern and when she could serve him coffee in it.

Jim in his chair saw her soft and happy face and felt contrite.

"I'm loaning those books to Annie Pomfrey," he said.

"That's nice," she said.

"She's studying by correspondence."

"She seems clever," she said.

She is so serene, he thought. Look at her hands, her beautiful hands. She never has to study, she does everything naturally. I've been so lucky.

He put down his cup and looked into the fire she had made with wood she had brought from the bush.

"It's a lovely fire," he said.

"Yes," she said staring dreamily into it.

He looked around the room.

"We'll have them over, don't you think?"

She smiled softly, beautifully, without looking at him.

"I think I can bear it," she said.

Maud was just ready when Vera came.

She (Maud) had just blown dust out of the teacups and set them back on their saucers when Vera's tap was heard on the door.

"I'm just ready!" Maud cried letting her in. "Just ready this very minute!"

She smiled a broad false-toothed smile on Vera who slid in and sat where she usually did close to the door. Maud fussed with the cushion behind her.

Dear me, she's depressed again, thought Maud feeling her own spirits rise.

She took her pleased face to the window and told herself she was allowing Vera a little time to recover.

There is something I'll point out to her, Maud thought with self congratulations on her generous nature.

"Look at the pretty flowers out in Mrs Morris's window box! They must have just come out. Violets they look like."

"I saw them this morning," Vera said, her broad flat face the colour of an old brown blanket with two raisins for eyes. She stood then sat again, a gesture of protest. "They're not violets. She poked some plastic flowers in among that green stuff. I wish you could've seen the violets I grew Maud."

Maud stood still her hands folded at her waist.

"There was this big rock at the back of the house," Vera said in a near trembling voice. "I grew the violets under it.

"It was cool and damp and I used to go at dusk every day and stand and smell."

Vera drew air into her nostrils and Maud did too.

"I'll get you a drink! I didn't offer you a drink when you came," Maud said when they had both exhaled.

She went briskly though an opening leading to a kitchen and returned with Vera's drink.

"And I didn't kiss you!" Maud said and kissed Vera over the glass of ginger beer causing the contents to wobble and almost spill on Vera's dress, a navy blue crepe patterned in brown, fraying around the buttonholes.

Vera took a sip of her drink and Maud watched her face for a change. There was none.

"I lost the house, you know Maud. It was in his name."

Maud knew. She gave her sitting room a brief but loving glance.

"I'll get myself a little drink too," she said and rose and did so.

They sipped alternately until Maud felt it was time to say something more.

"Irene should be in presently," she said.

"She still got her rat?" Vera said a thin stream of envy running into her mournful voice.

They both glanced at the floor and Maud who was quite proud of her slim feet in their medium heel beige shoes lifted them and folded one behind the other resting only one toe on the floor.

Vera lifted her feet too. She wore large boat-shaped shoes, some of the creases breaking into cracks and bulbous where her corns had taken over their shaping. She too placed one upon the other ready at a given moment to climb the chair leg.

Maud smiled a very tolerant smile.

"I saw her on the stairs yesterday and she said she couldn't sleep the night before and when she put the light on there it was sitting up looking at her.

"It made no attempt to go back into the hole, she said."

Maud and Vera looked stealthily around the visible areas of Maud's skirting board.

"We mustn't tell Mabel," said Maud.

She put a thumb under her chin pushing it upwards looking wisely on Vera.

"Mabel talks to Henderson."

"Runs after Henderson!" corrected Vera. There was the bark of a fox in her voice. Indeed she looked a lot like a large navy blue fox with age squashing its features and straggling its coat.

She tossed her head and opened her mouth as if she was ready to snap her jaws on Henderson, caretaker of the flats where they lived.

Her eyes strayed to the floor and so did Maud's and stayed there until there was a tap on the door.

Both jumped and swept their legs upwards.

"Oh dear," said Maud recovering first and standing up she smoothed down her dress and her hair even sweeping both hands down her cheeks.

She opened the door to Irene.

Irene sidled in.

She was unmarried while Vera was divorced Mabel widowed and Maud married to Bert not yet retired who worked as a storeman in a firm in the city.

Irene was long like a pencil with a small round head at one end and surprisingly big feet at the other. She had been tall and hard and skinny in her youth while other girls were rosy, warm and fleshy. The result was that Irene bent herself sideways in an attempt to shorten herself on one side at least. She remained bent in her old age and looked like a dandelion weathered by rain and wind with its head gone colourless and tufty. Irene had taken lately to hiding her colourless and tufty hair under an ancient dusty straw hat with a mauve flower made of some faded flimsy material sitting above her forehead.

Irene's face beamed under the flower with a sort of shy and ugly radiance.

"You look so happy dear!" Maud cried watching her while she seated herself sideways on a settee.

"Doesn't she look happy Vera?" said Maud.

"She's got her rat!" said Vera with a short sharp bark.

"Oh Maud," Irene said, "I left the light on last night and out he came—here I am saying 'he'."

"We always say 'he'," Vera said, "God knows why but we always say 'he'!"

"I shouldn't be saying 'he' Maud," said Irene, "Because it raised itself up Maud—"

Irene raised her two hands like the front paws of a rat and Maud and Vera looked around their feet and lifted them clear of the floor.

"And I saw these little pink titties! Little pink titties peeping out of the white fur!" said Irene. "Maud it was trying to tell me something."

"Well, it better not tell Henderson!" said Vera.

"We're keeping it from Mabel," said Maud running her eyes over the floor before fixing them on the bobbing flower on Irene's hat. "In case she lets something drop."

"Before the rat does!" cried Vera looking for the first time almost pleased.

"I'll get Irene a drink," said Maud getting up and bringing it from the kitchen.

"And I didn't kiss her!" she said wisely crushing a cheek against the flower before putting the glass into Irene's agitated hands.

Irene held her drink on her lap with a fixed expression ahead of her and the hint of a smile causing Maud and Vera to nervously follow her gaze.

Maud cleared her throat.

"We're not saying anything to Mabel dear," she said speaking louder than necessary. "Because she talks to Henderson and might say something."

"You can't bring anything into this place!" said Vera.

"I didn't bring it here," said Irene. "It might have been here first!"

"The notice says no pets of any kind," said Maud.

"No dogs!" said Vera.

"No cats!" said Maud.

"No caged birds!" said Vera.

"No pot plants on concrete surfaces!" said Maud.

"No climbing plants in window boxes!" said Vera. "No rats! Certainly no rats!" There was something close to relish in her voice.

Irene whose eyeballs swam in some colourless liquid like pale brown glue gripped her drink harder and was gripping it when Mabel knocked on the door.

"Mabel, oh Mabel!" cried Maud in greeting as Mabel came in large and showily dressed in tan coloured jersey splashed all over with huge flowers pale pink in colour and sprouting centres that ran into the hemline and the edge of her sleeves finishing at the elbows. She had a large head with frizzy gingerish hair making it appear larger and her shoes were freshly caked with white cleaner.

Vera who hadn't cleaned her shoes backed them under her chair.

"She's got her hibiscus dress on!" cried Maud. "We all love Mabel's hibiscus dress!

"And she's brought the deaths! Oh thank you dear!"

Maud kissed Mabel remembering this time to do it at once something which caused Vera's raisin eyes to flash into hard little currants.

Mabel had a folded paper under an arm which she went to put on a little table near Vera then decided not to.

It was the section of a daily newspaper that contained the columns of death notices.

Mabel confiscated this when a tenant on her floor separated it from the news section and dumped the unwanted pages into a receptacle left for waste paper.

None of them bought a daily paper although Maud's Bert read one for free at his works.

Maud took the paper from Mabel and Mabel took the chair that appeared to be waiting for her and laid her large flowery arms along the chair arms.

Maud without her glasses held the paper at arms' length squinting and grimacing as if this would help her eyesight, then tucked it under her arm.

"I'll see them later! I'll get Mabel her drink!"

Vera put up a hand.

"I'll have a look!"

She raised the paper which she read easily without glasses and Mabel looked hard at the back of it.

"Put it where Maud can find it easy!" said Mabel loudly as if the paper was a wall she had to shout through.

Maud bringing Mabel a drink gave her a soothing smile which Vera saw while folding the paper.

"Anyone there we know dear?" said Maud with a little soothing smile to Vera which Mabel also saw.

"No one there I'd like to be there if you know what I mean!" said Vera.

Maud arranged her features sympathetically.

103

"Would they come to the funeral if I died before them?" Vera said. "Would he come by himself? Would she come? I wonder!"

"They mightn't know," said Mabel.

"Of course they'd know!" said Vera the bark back in her voice. "Everyone's death goes in the death columns, doesn't it Maud?"

"I would think so dear," said Maud taking biscuits from a barrel and arranging them in a pattern on a plate. "What about the door? Shall we open it a little for Mabel to hear her phone if it rings?"

"Mabel's phone never rang once since we've been coming to Maud's on a Thursday!" barked Vera. "We could be blown to the GPO but the door has to be left open for Mabel's phone!"

Maud with some hesitancy opened the door a couple of inches.

"There! That shouldn't worry anyone!"

Irene's eyes full of watery dreams fixed themselves on the opening at floor level.

Maud looked down at her feet and moved them and Vera lifted hers.

Mabel looked down at her caked footwear and smoothed a hibiscus on her thigh.

"There has to be someone to put your death notice in the paper. It doesn't get there by itself does it Maud?" Mabel said. (Mabel had a married daughter living in the country.)

"He would put it in! I know he would!" said Vera.

"How would he know you died?" said Mabel. "He'd have to find out first." Her eyes were gingerish like her hair and they flashed from Vera to Maud.

"They're pretty busy with their little place. I doubt they'd even have time to read your name in the deaths let alone put it there. What do you say Maud?"

Maud was moving four cups and saucers on the cloth worked by herself for her glory box when she first met Bert.

She paused and like Irene assumed a dreamy air. Bert was several years younger so it was likely she would die first. She pictured his droopy face above some papers he was shuffling looking for her full name.

"Maud Florence!" she said suddenly into the silence and Vera jumped and looked at her feet.

"Oh, dear," Maud said going red.

"How would you know they're busy, Mabel?" said Vera as if gnawing a bone she was reluctant to put down. "You don't have to pass there to go to Dr Powers! You go the back way by Railway Street. It's shorter!"

"I can go to Dr Powers whatever way I like, Vera," said Mabel. "Anyway I made a special trip to have a look at the little place."

Vera for the moment could not raise a bark.

"They were busy too," said Mabel.

"When?" said Vera.

"Friday if you must know."

"You can't take any notice of Friday trade. All pubs are busy on a Friday! On other days there wouldn't be a soul there," said Vera.

"Well there was plenty of souls there when I looked in," said Mabel. "It was early in the day too. I saw her. She was flat out behind the bar. She had her hair all done up. Bouffant I think they call it. It looked real nice."

Maud stood.

"I'll put the jug on shall I?" she said.

Mabel mesmerized Maud to stillness with her eyes.

"They were busy when you and Bert were there, weren't they Maud?" Mabel said.

"You've never been there, Maud!" cried Vera.

"Oh yes she has," said Mabel. "Maud had a little stickybeak just like I did. Bert too!"

"Talk about rats!" cried Vera.

Irene grasped her bony knees in agitation and Maud sat suddenly lifting her feet from the floor. Vera looked wildly around the skirting board before finding Maud's face.

"Bert and I just took a little walk and when we were passing there Bert felt thirsty," Maud said her corseted body upright.

"Ryan's is across the road and Tattersall's next door! Why didn't you go there?"

"Bert wasn't thirsty then," said Maud.

106

"He got his thirst up in a hell of a hurry!" cried Mabel.

Maud reached out a hand and laid it on the ginger beer bottle.

"Have another little drink, Vera."

"No thank you Maud! You bought that drink from them! Did you?"

"Of course I don't buy drink anywhere but the supermarket!" said Maud.

"You left them a tip, I suppose! To pay for her bouffant hairdo!"

"Of course not, Vera! Bert never tips!"

After a moment Maud looked Irene's way and gave her a small anxious smile. "You all right there, dear?" she said.

"She's all right!" cried Vera and lifted her feet so that they looked like a pair of boats about to start in a race against each other.

Maud raised hers too leaving the tips of her toes barely touching the floor.

Mabel glanced from one pair of feet to the other and looked around her own two great white blobs on Maud's carpet.

Irene's feet remained glued to the floor and her eyes on the thin opening at the doorway.

Maud followed her gaze and half rose.

"Perhaps we could close the door while we have our tea?"

"Close it if you want to! Don't worry about me!" cried Mabel.

"I do worry about you Mabel," Maud said. "I worry about all of you."

"You worry about me all right!" said Vera.

"I worry about you most of all, Vera!" Maud said.

"Well thanks very much but don't worry about me!" said Vera.

"We're all like sisters. I say that all the time," said Maud.

Mabel lifted her arms from the chair arms and dropped them over the side where they hung like two huge floral bats.

"You said it last Wednesday in the queue for the matinee," Mabel said. "You said 'you and I are like sisters, Mabel. We're even closer than sisters!'"

"Youse went to the pictures!" cried Vera darting her eyes from one to the other and seeing Maud lower her eyes and Mabel wave her sleeves.

"We were all in here last Thursday and youse had been to the pictures the day before and not a word was said! Did Irene go?"

Irene did not shake her head. She didn't need to. Her beatific gaze was fixed on the pencil of light through the doorway. Maud and Vera looked too and lifted their feet.

Angrily Vera clamped hers down and Maud jumped.

"Dear me," she said looking around the floor.

"Dear me all right!" cried Vera. "Do you know what I did on Wednesday afternoon?" She plunged inside the neck of the navy blue crepe for a handkerchief and blew her nose. "I sat by the window and watched the bloody traffic go by! That's what I did!"

"It wasn't that much of a programme, was it Mabel?" Maud said.

Mabel swung her bat like arms up and down and arranged a small smile on her face.

"We thought of asking you to come along," said Maud. "Didn't we Mabel?"

"I don't remember if we did," said Mabel opening and shutting her little ginger eyes.

"Irene's not getting upset about it," said Maud with a soothing little smile taking in both Irene and Vera. "Are you dear?"

"She wouldn't be upset!" said Vera. "She'd be busy rat sitting!"

"What rat sitting?" cried Mabel lifting her feet so suddenly and violently some of the white flaked off her shoes and scattered on the floor.

"Irene's got a rat!" said Vera. "Hasn't she Maud?"

Maud wet her lips and looked towards the kitchen where the electric jug should be plugged in, avoiding Mabel's snapping accusing eyes.

"Maud knows about Irene's rat," said Vera with great calm and only a cursory look around the skirting board and her feet just clear of the floor.

Mabel raised her feet and wound them around the legs of her chair. The white cleaner streaked the brown polished wood.

"Oh, Mabel my best chair!" cried Maud. "I'll have to get that off before Bert gets home!" She moved forward as if to go at once for a cleaning cloth but sat back and lifted her feet an inch or two from the floor.

Mabel leaned back and rolled her ginger head on the chair back.

"Oh dear that sounds so funny!" she said stretching both legs out with her feet well above the floor.

Maud's eyes clung to Mabel's closed eyes.

Then she opened them and leaned foward.

"Tell Bert I marked the chair, Maud! He won't mind!"

"You don't know my Bert, Mabel!" Maud cried.

"Don't say 'my Bert' Maud! It might become a habit. And habits are hard to break!" Mabel with her large arms loose over the chair arms rolled her head from side to side, her eyes closed again.

Maud had gone white.

Vera saw and put her head back too and laughed raising her feet with abandon and clapping her boat shoes together.

"There's more than one rat scuttling about the building!"

"My little rat doesn't scuttle anywhere! He just comes to me!" Irene cried.

"It's a 'she' don't forget!" said Vera.

Irene intending to lean forward towards Mabel jerked sideways until she hung over the edge of the settee. She addressed the corner of the room past Mabel's chair.

"Don't tell Henderson! Don't tell Henderson!"

Mabel's hibiscus sleeve fell back to her elbow when she lifted an arm and looked with meditation on a raised hand quite well shaped with nails painted Maud noticed with a wildly beating heart.

"Come to think of it Bert doesn't scuttle about the building either," Mabel said. "He just comes to me!"

"Oh Mabel, he doesn't!" Maud cried out. "How can you be sure, Mabel?"

Maud looked wildly around her. "Bert goes to work and comes home!"

"So you say Maud," said Mabel placidly looking at her hand again.

"Oh Mabel, stop joking!" Maud went to stand then sat and looked around her feet as if in search of something but she had forgotten what.

"It's no joke," said Mabel. "You can't watch Bert every minute of the day Maud." She paused blinked her eyes rapidly. "Or night."

"Bert sleeps in his bed all night!"

"All night?"

"He gets up with his bladder! I hear him!"

"You hear him get up *or* go back to bed Maud. Not both."

"Mabel, stop it!" Maud cried getting up and briefly glancing at her ankles before returning her wide and blazing eyes to Mabel.

"Bert wouldn't hurt anyone! I know he wouldn't!"

"He certainly doesn't hurt me, Maud," said Mabel. "Quite the opposite."

"Oh my God!" shrieked Vera rocking herself with delight. "This is better than the pictures! I didn't miss anything after all!"

"She's joking. She's never met Bert!" said Maud.

"You hustle us out of here every Thursday before Bert gets home," Mabel said. "You don't want us to meet him, do you Maud?"

Maud took a pace or two towards Mabel but stopped before she could stand over her. She did not look at her feet.

"Get out of my house!"

Mabel stood both hands brushing down in a flowing movement her hibiscus dress.

"That's right! Say 'my house', Mabel! It's a good start!"

"Get out!" cried Maud.

"I'm going," said Mabel.

"Surely not before you've made a date for the pictures!" cried Vera, but she too was on her feet and just behind Maud when she flung the door open.

They went into the hall with Irene behind when Henderson came towards them on one of his routine inspections of the building.

Maud as if in a race against Mabel cried out: "There's a rat in the building, Mr Henderson!"

No one spoke although Irene was about to. Her gnarled purple hand crushed to her mouth caused nothing to emerge but a thin squeak.

They all leapt and looked at their feet. Henderson had trouble with his legs and they creaked and wavered while his trousers always worn too long seemed in danger of tangling him up.

"It's in Miss Crump's flat, Mr Henderson!" Maud cried. "It's upsetting us all, isn't it Mabel? But Mr Henderson will get rid of it, won't you Mr Henderson?"

But Mabel's head was up and her back towards them sailing away like a floral boat in the direction of her door.

The girl Tad who was nine came into the kitchen and saw her mother ironing.

The sight made her drop her schoolcase with a thud and think of running back and telling her brother Paddy.

He was rolling in a patch of dirt beside the verandah with the dog, a mongrel with a creamy grey coat patched with tan and eyes that apologized for his lowly state.

"Look at the mongrel!" the father had said more than once. "A rump like a wallaby and front paws like a blasted bandicoot!"

The dog rolled eyes desperate with shame, begging the father not to put him out of the kitchen if it was where Paddy and Tad were.

Paddy and Tad (shortened from Tadpole the nickname she got when she was born with a large head and body that whittled away to tendrils with feet on the end) wanted to get between the father and the dog to save it further hurt.

Foolishly the dog would make a squeak of protest which angered the father more.

"Get him out!" the father would say with a swing of his boot sending the dog up the steps—for the kitchen was on a lower level to the rest of the house—yelping and slunking for the patch beside the verandah where it usually lay in wait for the children.

Paddy was now having a glorious reunion with it, his shirt open and dust all over his pants. They snuffled and snorted and murmured and squeaked and it was hard to tell which noise came from the dog and which from the boy.

Tad went to the table and put her chin on the edge squeezing her eyes shut waiting for her mother's kiss.

There was the smell of heat and scorch and beeswax in the air.

Tad opened her eyes after a while and the mother was spreading an old work shirt of the father's on the ironing sheet.

Her face was shut like a window and her mouth not a kissing mouth.

But her hair was pretty with little gold springs near her ears and temples.

Tad ran a hand down a waterfall of tapes on a stack of ironed pillowslips.

"Don't rumple them up!" the mother said sharply.

Tad saw one of her play dresses looking only partly familiar with the sash ironed flat and the faded parts showing more than before. She went to go out to Paddy and the dog but only got to the door because the mother made a noise and Tad turned and saw her face with the eyes large and round and very blue.

"I'll do this damned ironing if it's the last thing I ever do!" she said.

Tad trailed back and sat on a chair.

"Where's Dad?" she said.

The mother snorted, picked up the father's shirt and flung it back into the old basket Paddy and Tad slept in as babies, now piled high all the time with wrinkled clothes. Tad noticed all the things in view in the basket seemed to be the father's.

The mother picked through the clothes and seemed to get angrier finding nothing but big shirts and rough old trousers.

"I'm not ironing another thing!" she said, and seizing the poker she slapped the irons on the stove sending them skidding to the back.

She sat down and drew a hand down her cheek leaving a black mark. She looked like a little girl who had played in the dirt at least no older than Mimi Anderson the big girl at school who sat by herself in the back seat. Often the teacher sat with her helping her with the hard work she did. No one was allowed to turn around and look.

Tad waited for the mother to say more.

"Your father made me do the ironing," she said.

This sounded strange to Tad.

"He rode over to McViety's this morning and had lemonade in their wash house!"

Tad felt her throat contract with a longing for lemonade. She and the mother looked at the stove where the kettle was sending out whispery grey breaths.

"There's no tea started," the mother said. "I can't even think what we'll have!"

"Stew with a crust?" Tad said, and knew at once it was a foolish suggestion.

On stew day the mother pushed the breakfast dishes back and threw the end of the tablecloth over them. She placed a large piece of quivering crimson meat on the bare table and cut it into little squares piling them on an old tin plate. If it wasn't school day Tad leaned over and watched, and unable to handle a sharp knife and squeamish at the feel of raw meat secretly worried about the time she would be married and want to feed her family stew and mightn't be able to.

The ironing was all over one end of the table now and a dish full of washing up at the other end so today was certainly not stew day.

The mother reached over for a clean handkerchief on the pile and blew her nose.

"Henry McViety built Dolly a shelf in the wash house and Henry showed it to your father." The mother tossed her head. "Dolly came along with a tray of cake and lemonade."

Tad wondered what kind of cake.

"I was here putting in a new row of beans," the mother said with a big tremble in her voice. "And then I had to nail two palings on the fence to stop the fowls from scratching the seeds out."

Tad wished for a big glass of lemonade for the mother when she was done.

"The stove was out and I had to build up the fire again."

There was the crunch of a big boot near the door and the father ducked inside because the door frame at that end of the kitchen wasn't high enough for him.

"The tadpole girl!" the father said. "Home from school!" He sounded more hearty than seemed necessary.

Tad didn't think she should kiss him since the mother hadn't kissed her. The father kept his eyes on Tad perhaps to avoid seeing the mother who laid a cheek on her hand with the handkerchief prominent.

"Mum did the ironing," Tad said. She looked at the basket. "Nearly all the ironing."

The father looked away quickly seeming to search for the dish on an iron frame in the corner under the tap, something he had arranged himself, setting up a small tank on a stand outside and bringing the tap inside by means of a hole cut in the kitchen wall. The children never tired of the story of how he did it as a surprise for the mother when she came home from hospital with Paddy as a baby.

He washed now with much sluicing and dried his hands the way he always did dragging the towel down each finger separately.

Tad wanted his cup of tea steaming on the table with a wedge of cake beside it, and couldn't look at the place where it should be.

Paddy came in and Tad knew by the scratching on the verandah boards the dog was coming too.

Paddy halted aware of the error and the dog compromising went and curled up under the safe where there was just enough room for him.

The father hung the towel up and sat down looking at the floor.

"Cowtime!" he said. "Tadpole and Paddymelon!"

The dog made a squeaking noise as if he wanted to be included. Paddy sitting on the step frowned a warning.

The father looked at the whispering kettle. Tad felt a corresponding dryness in her throat.

"Cowtime!" he said again, slapping both hands on his thighs. The dog raised his head and gave a yelp.

The mother blew her nose again. "Help me put the ironing away, Patrick and Freda," she said. The children felt a chill at the unfamiliar sound of their real names. The dog uttered a low growl reserved for strangers.

The father looked about him. "I might have a drink of water, eh Tadpole?"

"I'll get it for you, Dad," Tad said.

"You were told to put the ironing away," the mother said standing up and putting her handkerchief into the neck of her dress as if she wanted it close at hand. "But of course we haven't got a lovely tidy linen press like Dolly McViety." She sniffed deeply and began to sort the ironing. "We haven't got a linen press at all."

"We've got the sheet drawer," Tad said.

This was the middle drawer of the old cedar chest of drawers reserved for the household linen but almost always empty because the sheets were brought in from the clothes line and put on the beds and tea towels and face towels plucked from the basket when they were needed.

"The knobs need fixing," Paddy said.

The father burst into a laugh which sounded strange in the kitchen.

The mother burst into tears.

The dog jumped up and squeaking and snuffling circled the floor as if it were a circus ring.

Paddy and Tad were torn between concern for the mother's tears and the dog who almost brushed the father's boots with its low slung belly.

"There's no beds made, no tea on—" the mother wept.

"Mum doesn't even know what we'll have," Tad said with tears in her eyes.

Paddy took an old bald tennis ball from his schoolbag and began to bounce it between his feet. The dog barked with every bounce so Paddy stopped and gripped the ball tightly between his hands.

Outside Strawberry leading the other cows home gave a low bellow.

The father winced as if he too had a full udder.

The mother sat on her chair again and wiped her cheek with her fingers spreading the black mark farther out.

Tad couldn't summon the courage to tell her, although the mother told her over and over to say if there was a black mark on her face from the poker or pots and pans encrusted with soot and grease. "You never know who might come," she would say meaning Dolly McViety or her brother Henry, the nearest neighbours and just about the only people to call without warning.

"We don't want to be finishing up in the dark, do we Paddy and Tad?" the father said.

121

The dog gave a low growl, appreciating the seriousness of this event.

The mother stood up, sniffed and tossed her head. "I have to clean up the wash house," she said. "I have to make it so neat you could do the washing in the middle of the night without a light. Or serve cake and lemonade there like Dolly McViety does."

The father said nothing.

"Lucky Dolly McViety," the mother said. "How long since we've had money to spare for a bottle of lemonade?"

Tad and Paddy had a vision of a marble wobbling at the top of a bottle of greenish-white lemonade sweating a little with cold. Saliva came into their mouths.

"Dolly made the lemonade from their lemons," the father said.

In the small silence the mother took an iron from the stove and an old piece of curtain from the basket.

"Our lemon tree never got a go on," Paddy said.

The mother swept the iron across the curtain making more tears in it.

She laid it folded on the bank of ironing.

"I'm supposed to make the lemon tree grow I suppose, on top of everything I have to do.

"Why didn't you marry Dolly McViety?" she said.

"Why didn't you marry Henry?" the father said.

Tad got up and went and sat close to her brother on the step. The dog with a squeak and a stretching of his jaws got up too and lay across their feet.

The mother took a fresh iron and held it near her cheek already hot and scarlet.

She began to iron the ironing sheet. Her eyes were cast down and the black showed up more. I should say something, Tad worried although the McVietys would hardly come at milking time.

"Dolly would be sitting in her front room now with her sewing," the mother said. "She never has to go to the yard."

The father looked at the wall outside of which the dairy was waiting.

"Henry would be there now with a big slab of Dolly's caraway cake under his belt," the father said.

"I can't imagine anyone eating my cake after Dolly's," the mother said.

"Henry would," the father said. "He wouldn't notice whether it was seeds or flies' legs he was eating."

The children moved closer together. They had a vision of Dolly and Henry as their mother and father. They saw themselves wandering through the scrupulous order of the McViety house. The dog as if bidding them goodbye forever laid his jaws on his paws with a low mournful cry.

"Henry said regards to your Mollie when I was leaving," the father said.

The mother might not have heard. She took an armful of ironing and walked to the other part of the house with it.

The father stared at the doorway over the children's heads. Bellows from other cows added to Strawberry's painful plea. The father winced.

"Those cows'll bust," he said.

He looked at Paddy and Tad. "All I said was Dolly was a wonderful housekeeper," he said.

The dog growled in fearful amazement that one could be so foolish.

The mother returned. She had wiped her face clean of the black smudge and it was all pink and gold and white. You could see the mark of a comb through her forehead full of wheat-coloured curls.

She went to the stove. There was a click as she lifted the metal lid of the teapot, and the sound of a stream of puffing water.

She tossed her head while she tossed away the pot holder.

"Henry McViety can keep his old regards," she said.

The father stood up. He closed one crinkling brown eye on Paddy and Tad.

Then he saw the dog.

His smile vanished.

"Get that mongrel out!" he cried. "How did it get in? Rump like a wallaby and legs like a blasted bandicoot! Get him out!"

He woke and saw the empty place in the bed and knew at once he should worry about it.

He turned over away from the sight and thought through his half sleep what she might be doing.

After a while he could bear it no longer and got up and went to the back of the house.

He dodged past chairs in the living room pulled to odd angles. There were toys on the floor, a cup half full of coffee near the leg of the television, a half-knitted garment near a pile of tangled wool.

In the kitchen he saw the toaster showing a line of scarlet and there was a smell of hot metal.

He snapped the power off and let himself out of the house standing in the bleak cold with the yard emerging from the morning fog equally bleak.

There was the clothes hoist and under it a hole dug in the clay. Nearby was a battered doll's pram and a cardboard carton on its side sheltering a few pieces of dolls' furniture. Everything looked colder and more neglected for its film of dew.

He felt eyes. He jumped and so did Mrs Lake next door who had pulled aside a branch of a cassia bush on her side to look at him there shivering in his pyjamas.

She dropped the branch pretending to look into the shrub.

He wanted to say, "Have you seen my wife?" but couldn't bring himself to.

He heard her stops going back onto her porch.

She stopped abruptly and into the silence called out: "Your wife's on the road there, Mr Benson."

He was as startled to hear her speak as to hear him addressed that way. Hardly anyone called him Mister.

"Thank you," he said his voice coming out in a croak and went back inside. It was time for him to shower for work.

He couldn't see any clean shirts so he wore the one from yesterday, pushing his tie up under the collar hoping to disguise the dark line from his neck.

He heard some tinkling and knew his wife was in the kitchen.

The door of the little girls' bedroom was shut and he felt relief that they were still asleep.

Should he waken and feed and dress them, he said to the growing fear in his eyes reflected in the mirror. He laid down the hairbrush and went and gently opened their door.

They were there, thank God! At first he thought the little one's cot was empty. But she was curled in a bottom corner with a large rag doll across her rump. He worried that the older one lying half on top of the bedclothes might be cold but he resisted the temptation to cover her and closed the door almost without a sound.

His wife passed him then in her old skimpy dress and cardigan.

Her thongs slap slapped into the bedroom and she shut the door. He felt over himself and yes he had his wallet. But no car keys.

He tapped the door gently with a knuckle and almost at once there was the noise of a lumpy body flung against it and the key turned in the lock.

I'll go in the bus he thought, staring at the little girls' door and willing them to safety behind it.

He went out the back again feeling that he should be carrying something but it was months since she had packed him a lunch.

Over the fence now clearly seen, Mrs Lake was bringing her milk in. Her face was more yellow in the reflected light from the cassia bush and her strange hair had patches of custard yellow showing through the grey.

127

"I'm locked out," Chris said. "My wife's in the shower and can't hear. I don't want to wake the girls." He was pleased with himself for lying so well.

Mrs Lake saw him skinny and fair in his trousers flared out from the knees covering most of his strange shoes round as tennis balls in front.

"Come in and ring up," she said. "She might hear that."

"Thank you," he said only glad because of something to do.

But her phone rang as she entered her front room.

"Excuse me," she said trying not to look important.

With the receiver to her ear she motioned him on to the kitchen.

There was a pan on the stove with some grease in it and some brown fragments from fried eggs. A pot on the stove bore the homely marks of dribbled coffee. Every home in the world is sane but mine, he thought.

Mrs Lake came in.

"It was my daughter. She got a bedspread off layby and wants me to go across and see it on the bed this morning." She simpered a little with embarrassment giving him such details. But her yellowy face was full of pride while her eyes avoided his. He thought she might be making a secret and satisfactory comparison between her daughter and his wife.

"Would you like to ring?" she said bustling about clearing the table as if a trifle ashamed she was not further advanced in her day's work.

She put her hands around the coffee pot. "I'll pour you out a cup," she said.

He didn't move and thought about not going to work but sitting down and asking her for help.

The hot coffee made his eyes water.

"Those little girls," she said with her back to him wiping down the sink. "The little one. She doesn't say anything but when she sees me she points her finger. Just points her finger." Holding the dishcloth Mrs Lake pointed her finger the way the child did.

"That's Heather," he said although Mrs Lake would have known because when they first came to live next door she and his wife talked to each other.

"What's the other one's name?" Mrs Lake said. He got the impression she didn't like the older girl so much.

"Trudy," he said.

He longed for her to say into the silence that she would take them with her to her daughter's who lived on the other side of the reserve.

The little one would point her finger at interesting objects in the bush like a horse that strayed there and half tame magpies. He pictured the peaceful scene of Mrs Lake and the little girls bobbing along the bush track and smiled as he set down his cup.

129

"Thank you. I'll go and get the bus," he said and screwed his wrist to look at the time but hadn't put his watch on.

"You'll get it," Mrs Lake said bustling ahead of him to the front having noticed his wrists blue with cold and that he was without a jacket.

"My car keys are inside unfortunately," he said to her back.

"The bus'll do only the damn thing doesn't always come," Mrs Lake said, "But it'll be here this morning."

It was as if she couldn't believe his bad luck could extend that far.

"Thanks, Mrs Lake," he said running down the steps.

"Goodbye, son," she called after him.

On the bus he dreamed he took the little girls in to her every day. He imagined her scooping them up in her arms loving them equally. He pictured them at the table with her bustling about talking to them while they ate. He moved himself and the girls into the Lakes' house. Mr Lake died he thought with no callous intent as he believed him to be more than sixty. The bus bumped on and the woman next to him glancing at his bony wrists on his kness pulled her mouth down when he sniffed deeply. I hope there is no drip he thought because he had no handkerchief. He put a hand to his nose and felt there was. The woman got up and took another seat.

It allowed him a window seat. He would leave the suburb (too far out) and he and Mrs Lake and the little girls would live in one of the houses flying past the bus. That one, he thought getting a good view of it because it was close by the last bus stop before the railway station. It had a yard at the side sloping down to a little creek. There was a low thick tree half way up the slope blobbed with ripe oranges. Perfect, he thought looking back when the bus moved on.

In the bustle of everyone getting out and the hiss of the train pulling in he was able to sniff deeply without detection and waggle his nose dry on his sleeve.

Passing through to his office he swooped an arm over a glass partition and plucked up some tissues from someone's box grateful for the feel of them on his nostrils.

A clerk named Gail was at his cabinet looking for a file, a paper cup of coffee in one hand and the fingers of the other sprayed out holding a cigarette.

"Hi there," she said. "Tim Thomas wants to cancel and I think Jack wants you to go and see him and see if you can change his mind." She shut the cabinet with a twist of her hip. "The best of British."

"I should ring home first," he said. But he only stared at the phone.

Gail stood looking at him, her face and slightly prominent teeth pushed forwards between the peaks of her heavy hair.

"Oh God, I forgot!" he said.

"What?" she said very interested.

"I came in the train. I got no car today. I couldn't—I mean it wouldn't—"

"You can take mine," she said taking keys from a deep skirt pocket and laying them on his blotter.

"Oh thanks," he said putting his hand over the keys as if they were her hand.

"Love," he said inside his throat not sure if she should hear.

She turned and went out with lowered lashes carrying her coffee with care.

He watched her back and thought of her moving in with him and the girls. He stripped her of her black jumper with the high collar touching her ears and put her in a flowered apron. He saw her putting the living room in order clearing the floor of toys with the little girls swooped on top of her.

She was laughing and trying to get free. The dinner table was set with table napkins at jaunty angles on bread and butter plates and silver winking and every now and again there was a gentle spit from meat roasting in the oven.

He saw them together putting the girls to bed and smelled the girls' clean hair and clean sheets. Later he closed the bedroom door on Gail and himself. Watching her while she tossed her hair back and sat down to work his eyes pulled her jumper down over her naked shoulders. His thighs strained inside his pants. Oh my God my God, he said inside him.

We would keep the two cars he thought driving hers towards Tim Thomas, New and Used Vehicles. No, we would sell one and have no debts. He steered his mind from the bills piled under and around the clock on the kitchen shelf.

Tim Thomas left him standing holding his plastic folder (there was nothing in it relating to this visit but he usually carried it) while he finished a conversation with another caller. He took his time staring at the tips of his shoes, waggling his hands inside his pockets and looking past the boy's cheek at the car posters on the wall.

Chris looked at the stairs going up to a flat over the premises. The door had a brass knocker and he pictured Gail again in her apron with a finger covered by a rag polishing away at the knocker. The little girls were pressed against her legs watching. Tim Thomas had given them the flat rent free in return for a little bit of caretaking at the weekend. The girls went to a nearby nursery school.

He and Gail took turns at delivering and collecting them. They kept both cars he decided now. Of course. The sale of the house at a very good price took care of all his outstanding debts.

Tim Thomas was ready for him.

"I told them I cancelled for this week. I got nothing new to advertise. I told 'em." He fiddled with papers on his desk and twisted about.

"I know," Chris said his eyes travelling up and down the stairs before returning to Thomas's putty coloured chin.

"It's OK, Mr Thomas," Chris said his voice gentle as a girl's. "I just called to see if we could help in any way at all."

"Well—" Thomas was unable to look into the boy's blue eyes. Suddenly he threw a pencil across his desk. "Damn it! I don't want to lose the space—"

Chris moved to go his eyes back on the brass knocker.

"I'll tell 'em. Thanks, Mr Thomas." He slipped out aware that Thomas was watching his back with dissatisfied eyes.

Back in his office he looked about wildly for telephone messages. There was nothing. But the phone looked as if its creamy ear could hold some dark and terrible secret.

It rang. He took it up, listened a while, said it was OK and laid it down.

Gail came in then and saw his large swimming eyes.

"That was Thomas," he said. "He told me down there he was taking the ad then rang to say he wouldn't."

"What a bastard!" Gail said putting a file back in his cabinet.

"Gail!" he said and her hair swung round followed by her face.

He looked at her without speaking straining his eyes against the tears.

A slow red ran into her face.

"Oh, the keys," she said picking them up from his blotter and going slowly out.

"Don't look now," she said to Karen the girl at the next desk. "But I just got the come on."

Karen did look. She was currently without a boyfriend.

"Not for me," Gail said. "A fruitcake for a wife and two kids!"

But when the red dye left her face her eyes were brighter.

He caught the train at five o'clock and then the bus which dropped him at a corner store three blocks from home.

He went in and picked a pack of sausages from a refrigerator and laid them with a carton of eggs on the counter.

A door behind the counter opened into the rear of the shop where the owners lived. They were a man and wife named Franks.

There was no light on but flames from a fire licked at a black grate. A fat ginger cat sat on an easy chair which sat on a hand hooked rug on linoleum. There was a table covered with an old-fashioned green fringed cloth.

He saw the little girls kneeling by the chair, each with a hand on the cat their tangled hair smooth with brush and comb.

He saw Gail come in (in the apron) with a basin of steaming soup and the girls leave the floor and stand by her peering into the basin.

He removed Mr Franks to hospital with a terminal illness. Mrs Franks unable to run the shop alone sold out cheaply and gratefully.

Gail was busy and happy all day. He saw the four of them while the shop was closed on a Sunday afternoon walking on the reserve linked by their outstretched arms.

He turned surprised to see the dying Mr Franks looking quite robust come through the front door stamping wet leaves from his feet. At the same time Mrs Franks came through the living room shadows up to the counter.

"I thought you'd be back," she said with irritation.

"I chased the siren down Cook Road and around into Regent Street . . ."

Regent Street. That was the boy's street. He laid his hand on the eggs and held them.

"Well, was it police, fire brigade, ambulance or what?" Still testy she dropped the boy's money in the till with a little clatter.

"It got away from me," said Mr Franks and he went with head down to stir some oranges in a wire basket and straighten the sign that said they were locally grown and cheap and moved from there to fuss with the magazine stand.

Chris took up his things and ran. She had burned the house down, he thought. My little girls are dead. He saw them outlined in flames beating at a window.

He pulled up panting at his gate and they were at the window. He saw their ecstasy when they saw him. The little one threw back her head and laughed and pointed. The older one's smile made her turned up nose turn up more. They jigged about as if they wanted to break through the glass to reach him.

They raced into the kitchen to meet him there, wrapping their arms around his trouser legs while he peeled the wrapping from the sausages and turned on the stove.

"The stove's a clock!" the little one screamed with laughter when the element began to tick.

He gave them a nurse on each hip moving to the doorway to steal a look into the living room. His wife was on the couch under a rug, her eyes on the television screen. Her heavy body was hidden and her hair spread on a cushion golden in the half light. Her face was turned from his but he saw her cheek fair and smooth as butter.

Moving back to the stove he set the girls gently down.

They brought her to the table while he served the eggs and sausages onto their plates.

They chewed in silence and he moved his eyes over her once or twice then back to his food.

He stripped her of the excess flesh and the old cardigan half falling off her shoulders.

He put her into a white blouse he always liked with a frill that brushed the points of her ears when she moved her neck.

He smoothed her hair and swept it into a knot on top of her head the way she always used to wear it.

He saw the backyard through the window not gloomy and barren but filled with flowerbeds and little waterfalls and stepping stones the way she planned to do it.

He saw a hose playing gently and a light shining through hanging ferns.

It was the water that did it. He had to excuse himself and leave the table and go and look for a handkerchief.

Lucy was a thin, wistful wispy child who lived with her mother and grandmother and had few moments in her life except a bedtime ritual which she started to think about straggling home from school at four o'clock.

Sometimes she would start to feel cheerful even with her hands still burning from contact with Miss Kelly's ruler, and puzzle over this sudden lifting of her spirits then remember there was only a short while left to bedtime.

She was like a human alarm clock which had been set to go off when she reached the gate leading to the farm and purr away until she fell asleep lying against her grandmother's back with her thighs tucked under her grandmother's rump and her face not minding at all being squashed against the ridge of little knobs at the back of her grandmother's neck.

Her grandmother and her mother would talk for hours after they were all in bed. Sometimes it would seem they had all drowsed off and the mother or the grandmother would say "Hey, listen!" and Lucy would shoot her head up too to hear. Her grandmother would dig her with an elbow and say: "Get back down there and go to sleep!" Lucy was not really part of the talk just close to the edges of it.

It was as if the grandmother and the mother were frolicking together in the sea, but Lucy unable to swim had to stand at the edge and be satisfied with the wash from their bodies.

Lucy made sure she was in bed before her mother and grandmother in order to watch.

It was as if she were seeing two separate plays on the one stage. Carrie the mother performed the longest. She was twenty-six and it was the only time in the day when she could enjoy her body. Not more than cleansing and admiring it since Lucy's father had died five years earlier. Carrie was like a ripe cherry with thick black hair cut level with her ears and in a fringe across her forehead. She was squarish in shape not dumpy or overweight and with rounded limbs brown from exposure to the sun because she and the grandmother Jess also a widow and the mother of Carrie's dead husband worked almost constantly in the open on their small farm which returned them a meagre living.

Carrie was nicknamed Boxy since she was once described in the village as good looking but a bit on the boxy side in reference to her shape. When this got back to Carrie she worried about it although it was early in the days of her widowhood and her mind was not totally on her face and figure.

Some time later at night with all her clothes off and before the mirror in the bedroom she would frown on herself turning from side to side trying to decide if she fitted the description. She thought her forehead and ears were two of her good points and she would lift her fringe and study her face without it and lift her hair from her ears and look long at her naked jawline then take her hands away and swing her head to allow her hair to fall back into place. She would place a hand on her hip, dent a knee forward, throw her shoulders back and think what a shame people could not see her like this.

"Not boxy at all," she would say inside her throat which was long for a shortish person and in which could be seen a little blue throbbing pulse.

She shook her head so that her thick hair swung wildly about then settled down as if it had never been disturbed.

"See that?" she would say to her mother-in-law.

Jess would be performing in her corner of the room and it was usually with a knee up under her nightdress and a pair of scissors gouging away at an ingrown toenail. She never bothered to fasten the neck of her nightdress and it was an old thing worn for many seasons and her feet were not all that clean as she did not wash religiously every night as Carrie did. She spent hardly any time tearing off her clothes and throwing them down, turned so that the singlet was on the outside and when she got into them in the morning she had only to turn the thickness of the singlet, petticoat and dress and pull the lot over her head.

Carrie did not seem to notice although she sometimes reprimanded Jess for failing to clean her teeth. When this happened Jess would run her tongue around her gums top and bottom while she ducked beneath the covers and Lucy would be glad there was no more delay.

It was only the operations like digging at a toenail or picking at a bunion that kept Jess up. Sometimes she pushed her nightdress made into a tent with her raised knee down to cover her crotch but mostly she left it up so that Lucy hooped up in bed saw her front passage glistening and winking like an eye.

The lamp on the dressing table stood between Carrie and Jess so that Lucy could see Carrie's naked body as well either still or full of movement and rhythm as she rubbed moistened oatmeal around her eyes and warmed olive oil on her neck and shoulders.

The rest of the little town knew about the bedtime ritual since Walter Grant the postmaster rode out one evening and saw them through the window. It had been two days of wild storms and heavy rain and the creek was in danger of breaking its banks. Any stock of Carrie's and Jess's low down would be safer moved. Walter on his mission to warn them saw Jess with her knee raised and her nightgown around her waist and Carrie's body blooming golden in the lamplight for they were enjoying the storm and had left the curtains open. Walter saw more when Carrie rushed to fling them together and rode home swiftly with his buttocks squeezed together on the saddle holding onto a vision of Carrie's rose tipped breasts, the creamy channel between them, her navel small and perfect as a shell and her thighs moving angrily and her little belly shaking.

After that the town referred to the incident as that "cock show".

Many forecast a dark future for Lucy witnessing it night after night.

Some frowned upon Lucy when she joined groups containing their children at the show or sports day.

The Lang women's house had only one bedroom, one of two front rooms on either side of a small hall. The hall ran into a kitchen and living room combined which was the entire back portion of the house.

It would have been reasonable to expect them to make a second bedroom by moving the things from what was called the "front room". But neither Jess nor Carrie ever attempted or suggested this. The room was kept as it was from the early days of Jess's marriage. It was crowded with a round oak table and chairs and a chiffonier crowded with ornaments, photographs and glassware and there were two or three deceptively frail tables loaded with more stuff. On the walls were heavily framed pictures mostly in pairs of swans on calm water, raging seas and English cottages sitting in snow or surrounded by unbelievable gardens.

Even when the only child Patrick was living at home and up until he left at fifteen he slept in the single bed in his parents' room where Carrie slept now. He was fifty miles up the coast working in a timber mill when he met Carrie a housemaid at the town's only hotel. They married when he was twenty and she was nineteen and pregnant with Lucy who was an infant of a few months when Patrick was loaned a new-fangled motor bike and rounding a bend in the road the bike smacked up against the rear of a loaded timber lorry like a ball thrown hard against a wall. Patrick died with a surprised look on his face and his fair hair only lightly streaked with dust and blood.

Jess was already widowed more than a year and managing the farm single handed so Carrie and Lucy without a choice came to live there.

Lucy could not remember sleeping anywhere but against her grandmother's back.

Sometimes when the grandmother turned in the night she fitted neatly onto the grandmother's lap her head on the two small pillows of her grandmother's breasts.

She was never actually held in her grandmother's arms that she knew about. When she woke the grandmother's place was empty because it was Jess who was up first to start milking the cows which was up to twenty in the spring and summer and half that in the winter. Carrie got up when the cows were stumbling into the yard seen in the half light from the window and Lucy waited about until eight o'clock when they both came in to get breakfast. Lucy was expected to keep the fire in the stove going and have her school clothes on. She usually had one or another garment on inside-out and the laces trailing from her shoes and very often she lied when asked by Carrie or Jess if she had washed. Carrie did little or no housework and Jess had to squeeze the necessary jobs in between the farmwork. Carrie was content to eat a meal with the remains of the one before still on the table, clearing a little space for her plate by lifting the tablecloth and shaking it clear of crumbs, sending them into the middle of the table with the pickles and sugar and butter if they could afford to have a pound delivered with their empty cream cans from the butter factory.

Carrie trailed off to bed after their late tea not caring if she took most of the hot water for her wash leaving too little for the washing up.

Jess grumbled about this but not to Carrie's face.

Once after Jess had managed on the hot water left and the washing up was done and the room tidied she said in Lucy's hearing that she hoped Carrie never took to bathing in milk.

Lucy had a vision of Carrie's black hair swirling above a tubful of foamy milk. Her own skin prickled and stiffened as if milk were drying on it. She left the floor where she was playing and put her chin on the edge of the table Jess was wiping down waiting to hear more. But Jess flung the dishcloth on its nail and turned her face to busy herself with shedding her hessian apron as the first step towards getting to bed.

This was the life of the Lang women when Arthur Mann rode into it.

Jess and Carrie inside following their midday meal saw him through the kitchen window with the head of his horse over the fence midway between the lemon tree and a wild rose entangled with convolvulus. The blue bell-like flowers and the lemons made a frame for horse and rider that Jess remembered for a long time.

"It's a Mann!" Jess said to Carrie who did not realize at once that Jess was using the family name.

The Manns were property owners on the outer edge of the district and they were well enough off to keep aloof from the village people. Their children went to boarding schools and they did not shop locally nor show their cattle and produce at the local show but took it to the large city shows.

But Jess easily recognized a Mann when she saw one. When she was growing up the Manns were beginning to grow in wealth and had not yet divorced themselves from the village. They not only came to dances and tennis matches but helped organize them and there were Manns who sang and played the piano in end-of-year concerts and Manns won foot races and steer riding at the annual sports.

They nearly all had straight dark sandy hair and skin tightly drawn over jutting jawbones.

Jess going towards the fence got a good view of the hair and bones when Arthur swept his hat off and held it over his hands on the saddle.

"You're one of the Manns," said Jess her fine grey eyes meeting his that were a little less grey, a bit larger and with something of a sleepy depth in them.

Arthur keeping his hat off told her why he had come. He had leased land adjoining the Langs' to the south where he was running some steers and he would need to repair the fence neglected by the owners and the Langs neither of whom could afford the luxury of well fenced land.

He or one of his brothers or one of their share farmers would be working on the fence during the next few weeks.

"We don't use the bit of land past the creek," said Jess before the subject of money came up. "The creek's our boundary so a fence is no use to us."

Arthur Mann's eyes smiled before his mouth. He pulled the reins of his horse to turn it around before he said there would be no costs to the Langs involved. He put his hat on and raised it again and Jess saw the split of his coat that showed his buttocks well shaped like the buttocks of his horse which charged off as if happy to have the errand done.

Jess came inside to the waiting Carrie.

Lucy home from school was playing with some acorns she found on the way. Jess saw her schoolcase open on the floor with some crusts in it and the serviette that wrapped her sandwiches stained with jam. Flies with wings winking in the sun crawled about the crusts and Lucy's legs.

"She's a disgrace!" Jess cried trying to put out of her mind the sight of Arthur Mann's polished boots and the well ironed peaks of his blue shirt resting on the lapels of his coat.

With her foot Carrie swept the acorns into a heap and went to the mirror dangling from the corner of a shelf to put her hat on. Jess took hers too from the peg with her hessian apron. She turned it around in her hands before putting it on. It was an old felt of her husband's once a rich grey but the colour beaten out now with the weather. It bore stains and blotches where it rubbed constantly against the cows' sides as Jess milked. Jess plucked at a loose thread on the band and ripped it away taking it to the fire to throw it in.

The flames snatched it greedily swallowing the grease with a little pop of joy.

Lucy lifted her face and opened her mouth to gape with disappointment. She would have added it to her playthings.

"Into the fire it went!" said Jess. "Something else you'd leave lyin' around!"

She looked for a moment as if she would discard the hat too but put it on and went out.

It was Carrie who encountered Arthur Mann first working on the fence when she was in the corn paddock breaking and flattening the dead stalks for the reploughing. Almost without thinking she walked towards the creek bank and stood still observing Arthur who had his back to her. He is a man, she thought remembering Jess's words with a different inference. His buttocks under old, very clean well-cut breeches quivered with the weight of a fence post he was dropping into a hole. He had his hat off lying on a canvas bag that might have held some food. Jess might have wondered about the food and thought of a large clean flyproof Mann kitchen but Carrie chose to look at Arthur's hair moving in a little breeze like stiff bleached grass and his waistline where a leather belt shiny with age and quality anchored his shirt inside his pants.

He turned and saw her.

As he did not have a hat to lift he seemed to want to do something with his hands so he took some hair between two fingers and smoothed it towards an ear. Carrie saw all his fine teeth when he smiled.

"Hullo . . . Shorty," he said.

"No . . . Boxy," she said.

She was annoyed with herself for saying it.

He probably knew the nickname through his share farmers who were part of the village life and would have filled the waiting ears of the Manns with village gossip. Carrie did not know but he had heard too about the nightly cock show.

Arthur thought now of Carrie's naked body although it was well covered with an old print dress once her best, cut high at the neck and trimmed there and on the sleeves with narrow lace. Carrie was aware that it was unsuitable for farm work and took off her hat and held it hiding the neckline. She shook her hair the way she did getting ready for bed at night and it swung about then settled into two deep peaks against her cheeks gone quite pink.

"Come across," said Arthur. "I'm stopping for smoko."

Carrie nearly moved then became aware of her feet in old elastic-side rubber boots and buried them deeper in the grass.

She inclined her head towards the corn paddock as if this was where her duty lay. Still holding her hat at her neck and still smiling she turned and Arthur did not go back to the fence until she had disappeared into the corn.

Carrie spent the time before milking at the kitchen table in her petticoat pulling the lace from the dress. Lucy home from school with her case and her mouth open watched from the floor. When Carrie was done she stood and pulled the dress over her head brushing the neck and sleeves free of cotton ends. She swept the lace scraps into a heap and moved towards the stove.

"Don't burn it!" Jess cried sharply. "Give it to her for her doll!"

Lucy seized the lace and proceeded to wind it around the naked body of a doll that had only the stump of a right arm, its nose squashed in and most of its hair worn off.

A few days later Arthur rode up to the fence with a bag of quinces.

Lucy saw him when she looked up from under the plum tree that grew against the wall of the house. She was on some grass browning in the early winter and her doll sat between her legs stuck stiffly out. Arthur raised the quinces as a signal to collect them but Lucy turned her face towards the house and Arthur saw her fair straight hair that was nothing like Carrie's luxuriant crop.

In a moment Carrie came from one side of the house and Jess from the other. They went up to the fence and Lucy got up and trailed behind.

Arthur handed the quinces between Carrie and Jess and Jess took them taking one out and turning it around.

She did not speak but her eyes shone no less than the sheen from the yellow skin of the fruit.

"The three Lang women," Arthur said smiling. "Or are there four?"

Lucy had her doll held by its one and a half arms to cover her face. Ashamed she flung it behind her back.

Arthur arched the neck of his horse and turned it around.

"I'll buy her a new one," he said and cantered off.

Neither Jess nor Carrie looked at Lucy's face when they went inside. Jess tipped the quinces onto the table where they bowled among the cups and plates and she picked one up and rubbed her thumb thoughtfully on the skin and then set it down and gathered them all together with her arms.

Then she went into the front room and returned with a glass dish and with the hem of her skirt wiped it out and put the fruit in and carried it back to set it on one of the little tables. Carrie's eyes clung to her back until she disappeared then looked dully on Lucy sitting stiff and entranced on the edge of a chair. She opened her mouth to tell Lucy to pick up her doll from the floor but decided Jess would do it on her return. But Jess stepped over the doll and put on her hessian apron and reached for her hat. She turned it round in her hands then put it back on the peg. Carrie saw the back of her neck unlined and her brown hair without any grey and her shoulders without a hump and her arms coming from the torn-out sleeves of a man's old shirt pale brown like a smooth new sugar bag. Then when Jess reached for an enamel jug for the house milk Carrie saw her hooded eyelids dropping a curtain on what was in her eyes. Carrie put her hat on without looking in the mirror and followed Jess out. She looked down her back over her firm rump to her ankles for something that said she was old but there was nothing.

In bed that night Lucy dreamed of her doll.

It had long legs in white stockings with black patent leather shoes fastened with the smallest black buttons in the world.

The dress was pink silk with ruffles at the throat and a binding of black velvet ribbon which trailed to the hemline of the dress. The face was pink and white and unsmiling and the hair thick and black like Carrie's hair.

Lucy lay wedged under the cliff of her grandmother's back wondering what was different about tonight. She heard a little wind breathing around the edges of the curtain and a creak from a floor-board in the kitchen and a small snuffling whine from their old dog Sadie settling into sleep under the house.

Lucy marvelled at the silence.

No one is talking she thought.

Every afternoon Lucy looked for the doll when she came in from school. On the way home she pictured it on the table propped against the milk jug, its long legs stretched among the sugar bowl and bread-crumbs.

But it was never there and when she looked into the face of Jess and Carrie there was no message there and no hope.

The following Saturday Lucy could wait no longer and sneaked past the cowyard where Jess and Carrie were milking and well clear of it ran like a small pale terrier through the abandoned orchard and bottom corn paddock to the edge of the creek. Across it, a few panels of fence beyond where Carrie had first encountered him, Arthur was at work.

Under her breath Lucy practised her words: "Have you brought my doll?"

She was saying them for the tenth time when Arthur turned.

She closed her mouth before they slipped out.

Arthur pushed his hat back and beckoned.

"Come over," he said.

Lucy hesitated and looked at her feet buried in the long wild grass. I won't go, she said to herself. But the doll could be inside Arthur's bag hung on a fence post.

She plunged down the creek bank and came up the other side her spikey head breaking through the spikey tussocks dying with the birth of winter.

Arthur sat down on some fence timber stewn on the ground and reached for his bag. Lucy watched, her heart coming up into her neck for him to pull the doll from it. But he took out a paper bag smeared with grease which turned out to hold two slices of yellow cake oozing red jam. When he looked up and saw the hunger in Lucy's eyes he thought it was for the cake and held it towards her.

"We'll have a piece each," he said.

But Lucy sank down into the grass and crossed her feet with her knees out. Then she thought if she didn't take the cake Arthur might not produce the doll so she reached out a hand.

"Good girl," he said when she began nibbling it.

The cake was not all that good in spite of coming from the rich Mann's kitchen. It had been made with liberal quantities of slightly rancid butter.

Lucy thought of bringing him a cake made by Jess and imagined him snapping his big teeth on it then wiping his fingers and bringing out the doll.

"I should visit you, eh?" Arthur said.

Oh, yes! He would be sure to bring the doll.

"When is the best time?" Arthur said folding the paper bag into a square and putting it back in his bag.

"At night after tea? Or do you all go to bed early?"

Lucy thought of Carrie naked and Jess with her legs apart and shook her head.

"Why not at night?" Arthur said. "There's no milking at night, is there?"

Lucy had to agree there wasn't with another small head shake.

"What do you all do after tea?" said Arthur.

Lucy looked away from him across the paddocks to the thin drift of smoke coming from the fire under the copper boiling for the clean up after the milk was separated. She felt a sudden urge to protect Jess and Carrie from Arthur threatening to come upon them in their nakedness.

She got to her feet and ran down the bank, her speed carrying her up the other side and by this time Arthur had found his voice.

"Tell them I'll come!" he called to her running back.

Carrie was in bed that night with much less preparation than usual and even without the last minute ritual of lifting her hair from her nightgown neck and smoothing down the little collar, then easing herself carefully down between the sheets reluctant to disturb her appearance even preparing for sleep.

To Lucy's surprise her nightgown hung slightly over one shoulder and she was further surprised to see that Jess had fastened hers at the brown stain where her neck met the top of her breasts. Carrie had not cavorted in her nakedness and Jess had not plucked at her feet with her knees raised. Lucy looked at the chair where Jess usually sat and pictured Arthur there. She saw his hands on his knees while he talked to them and curved her arms imagining the doll in them. An elbow stuck into Jess's back and Jess shook it off.

"Arthur Mann never married," said Carrie abruptly from her bed.

Jess lifted her head and pulled the pillow leaving only a corner for Lucy who didn't need it anyway for she had raised her head to hear.

"Old Sarah sees to that," said Jess.

Before putting her head down again Lucy saw that Carrie was not settling down for sleep but had her eyes on the ceiling and her elbows up like the drawing of a ship's sail and her hands linked under her head.

Jess's one open eye saw too.

Lucy had to wait through Sunday but on Monday when she was home from school for the May holidays she slipped past the dairy again while Jess and Carrie were milking and from the bank of the creek saw not only Arthur but a woman on a horse very straight in the back with some grey hair showing neatly at the edge of a riding hat and the skin on her face stretched on the bones like Arthur's. The horse was a grey with a skin like washing water scattered over with little pebbles of suds and it moved about briskly under the rider who sat wonderfully still despite the fidgeting.

157

Lucy sank down into the tussocks on the bank and the woman saw.

"What is that?" she said to Arthur. Then she raised her chin like a handsome fox alerted to something in the distance and fixed her gaze on the smoke away behind Lucy rising thin and blue from the Lang women's fire.

Lucy had seen Arthur's face before the woman spoke but he now lowered his head and she saw only the top of his hat nearly touched the wire he was twisting and clipping with pliers.

The horse danced some more and Lucy was still with her spikey head nearly between her knees staring at the ground. The woman wanted her to go. But Lucy had seen people shooting rabbits not firing when the rabbits were humped still but pulling the trigger when they leapt forward stretching their bodies as they ran. Perhaps the woman had a gun somewhere in her riding coat and breeches or underneath her round little hat. Lucy sat on with the sun and wind prickling the back of her neck.

"Good heavens!" the woman cried suddenly and wheeling her horse around galloped off.

Lucy let a minute pass then got up and ran down and up the opposite bank to Arthur.

He went on working snip, snip with the pliers until Lucy spoke.

"You can come of a night and visit," she said.

Arthur looked up and down the fence and only briefly at the Lang corn paddock and the rising smoke beyond it.

"I've finished the fence," he said.

Lucy saw the neat heap of timber not needed and the spade and other tools ready for moving. She saw the canvas bag on top, flat as a dead and gutted rabbit.

"I know why you didn't bring the doll," she said. "Your mother won't let you."

Mother and the five children were around the table for midday dinner one Saturday in the spring of 1930.

Mother had passed out the plates of potato and pumpkin and corned beef except Father's, and the children anxious to start kept looking at the kitchen door.

"Now everyone behave when Father comes," Mother said, her dull blue eyes skimming over them all without resting on anyone, even Tom.

But the children's eyes, from twelve year old Fred to Rosie the baby swung towards Tom next in age to Fred. Tom lifted a shoulder and rubbed it around his ear.

"Tom's doing it, Mother," said Letty.

Mother was about to tell Tom not to, because the habit irritated Father, and Lord knows what it might lead to when the door opened and Father was there.

"There you are, Lou," said Mother bustling to the old black stove and taking his dinner from the top of a saucepan she set it in his place.

Father hooked his old tweed cap on the back of his chair and fixed his eyes on Rosie, who was in her highchair with her head tipped back and her blue eyes glittering with the brilliance of her smile for him that showed every one of her pearly teeth.

"That cheeky one will get a hiding before the day is out," said Father sitting down.

Fred, Letty and Grace laughed because it was wise to laugh when Father joked and the idea of Father's favourite, beautiful innocent four year old Rosie being belted with the leather strap was quite laughable.

Mother sent a small smile Father's way thanking him for his good humour. Tom was opposite Father and Father fixed his brown eyes suddenly gone hard on him, because Tom, lifting a shoulder again and rubbing it around his ear, hadn't laughed.

Tom had stolen a look at the strap hanging behind the kitchen door. It surprised him the way things were always being lost in and around the house but the strap, long and broad and shining and curled a little at one end, never strayed from its nail except when it was flaying the air and marking the children's legs, nearly always Tom's, with pink and purple stripes.

Tom felt his legs prickle at the sight of it. The old clock on the dresser with a stain in its face where

Mother had poured separator oil into the works to get it going showed one o'clock. Tom dropped his knife and fork and counted on his fingers under the table. Two, three, four and up to eight o'clock when everyone was sent to bed.

Could he stay out of trouble that long? There were once ten Saturdays in a row when Tom got a hiding. As soon as Saturday dawned the topic was whether Tom would get a hiding before the day was out. Tom ashamed and fearful would lift his shoulder to his ear and wish for time to race away as fast as old Henry the cattle dog fled for the safety of the corn paddock from Father's blucher boot.

Tom was wishing that now, counting carefully with both hands from one to eight. He was slow at school, in the same class with Letty two years younger, so it took him a long time. Father saw Tom's lips moving and not with pumpkin and potato behind them. Rancour rose inside Father churning at his innards and making him stand his knife and fork upright beside his plate with a noise like bullets from a double barrelled gun. The young whelp! The dingo! Neglecting food slaved for under the hot sun and orders barked out by old Jack Reilly on whose farm Father did labouring work because his own place couldn't keep the seven of them. Seven! My God, he should be free to go to Yulong races this afternoon with money in his pocket and an oyster coloured felt

162

hat, a white shirt and a red tie. He clenched his jaws on the tough meat and snapped his head back, eyes with the whites showing fixed on Tom.

"You!" he yelled and everyone jumped. "You! Eat up! Eat up or I'll skin the hide off you! I'll beat you raw as a skinned wallaby! S-s-s-s-s—" When angry Father made a hissing noise under his tongue that was more ominous than a volume of words. Knives and forks now clattered vigorously on the plates.

"Eat up, everyone," said Mother hoping to pull Father's eyes away from Tom.

"Everyone is eating up except Tom," Grace said looking at Father for approval.

Father held Tom's mesmerized eyes. "Up straight in your chair!"

Tom took up his knife and fork and glanced down at the wooden bench he shared with Fred and Grace.

"It's not a chair," he said. "It's a stool."

Even to his own ears the words sounded not his own. They were his thoughts and they had rushed from him like air from a blown balloon pricked with a pin. Perhaps he only thought he said them. He looked around the table and saw by the shocked faces that he had. Then he saw Father, who was long and lean and sinewy, grow longer as he reared up above the table. Tom scarcely ever thought of more than one thing at once. Now he only thought how much Father reminded him of a brown snake.

Father dropped his knife and fork with a terrible clatter and seized Tom by his old cambric shirt. There was the noise of tearing.

"Oh, Lou!" Mother cried with a little moan. "Don't Lou!"

"Don't Lou!" said Father mocking her. "Won't Lou! I'll kill him!"

Father had risen from his chair and it fell backwards onto the floor.

"I'll pick up Father's chair," said Letty looking at everyone and anticipating their envy because she thought of it first.

"I'll get the strap," said Grace feeling she had gone one better.

Father let go Tom's shirt but held onto him with his eyes, his body hooped over the enamel milk jug and the tin plate of bread.

Tom saw Father's red neck running down inside his unbuttoned grey flannel.

He's like a red bellied snake, Tom thought and the corner of his mouth twitched.

"Oooh, aah," cried Letty aghast. "Tom's grinning!"

She was on one side of Father having put the chair upright Grace was on the other side holding out the strap. The only sound was the busy ticking of the clock.

Rosie spoke first. "I love Tom!" she cried.

Eyes swung to Rosie and breaths were let out in shocked gasps.

The words had rushed from the small, sweet, red mouth the way Tom's words had. Rosie too seemed shocked at herself and looked around the table, pressing the spoon to her mouth as if to hold back more.

Eyes flew to Father. What would happen now? But Father still held Tom by the eyes, one hand groping in the air for the strap.

"Here it is, Father," said Grace and Letty moved Father's chair to make it easier for him to make his way around the table.

"Finish up your dinner first Lou, while it's hot!" Mother urged.

Father began to lower himself slowly towards his chair.

He's going back into his hole, Tom thought and his mouth twitched again.

Eyes were on Tom so no one could shriek a warning when Father lowered himself past his chair and hit the floor with a thud.

"Oh, Lou!" Mother cried out. "Lou, are you hurt?"

"Poor Father!" cried Letty, anxious to shift any blame from herself. "It's all Tom's fault!"

Mother helped Father up, pressing him into his chair deliberately cutting off his vision of Tom. If Mother's back could have spoken it would have said Run Tom, run. Go for your life. If he hits you now he might kill you. Run, run. Please run.

"Finish up your dinner first Lou," Mother said.

Father sat with the strap across his lap.

Suddenly Rosie cried out, "Don't hit Tom!"

Oh my goodness, said the breaths jerking from Mother, Grace, Letty and Fred. Father would hear this time!

Father did. His head snapped back as he reared up. He swung the strap around the table like a stockwhip, flicking Rosie's cheek and missing Fred who was skilful at ducking. The strap wrapped itself with stinging force around Tom's neck. Without a sound he leaped from the stool, sailed across the corner of the table and out through the kitchen door leaving it swinging behind him. Even before Rosie started to scream they heard the rustling of the corn as Tom fled through it.

"Oooh, aah," cried Letty and Grace scuttling back to their places on either side of the shrieking Rosie.

Rosie had flung her head over the back of her chair.

Her eyes were screwed tight and tears ran down her face over the three cornered white mark rapidly cutting into the pink of her cheek.

"Fred should go after Tom, shouldn't he Father?" Letty shouted above the noise.

"Father only meant to hit Tom, didn't you Father?" shouted Grace.

Father took up his knife and fork again. This uncaring gesture caused Rosie to shriek louder.

Father cut savagely into his meat. Rosie leaned towards Grace for comfort but Grace frightened at

Father's profile jerked away from her. The pitch of Rosie's scream increased. Mother got up and filled the teapot at the stove.

"Your tea's coming Lou," she shouted.

The cruelly unloved Rosie stretched both arms across the tray of her highchair. Father dropped his knife and fork, seized the strap and slapped it hard across her arms.

She bellowed now like a young calf and flung the wounded arms towards Fred. But Fred pulled himself away from her and made chewing motions without swallowing, keeping his eyes on his plate. "Take her outside," said Mother to Letty and Grace.

Grace lifted a stiffened Rosie from her chair and bore her out with Letty trotting alongside. Rosie's arms now marked identically to her cheek, stretched piteously over Grace's shoulder towards Mother.

"Go after that animal," said Father to Fred. "And bring him back for me to belt the daylights out of him."

"Yes, Father," said Fred and left the table. He began to run before he reached the kitchen door.

Father's eyes bored into Mother's plate with so little of her food eaten. She began at once sawing into her meat.

"I baked a batch of brownies this morning, Lou," she said. "I'll get you one while they're all away."

But Letty and Grace were in the doorway, Rosie in Grace's arms. Rosie's hair was damp with sweat, her face scarlet. Hiccuping she looked pathetically towards Father. Grace set her down on the floor.

"Rosie has something to tell Father," Grace said.

"Go on Rosie," Letty said, giving her a little push.

Rosie stuck half a hand in her mouth and stared at the floor. After a moment she removed the hand and cried out "I hate Tom!"

Father stopped chewing and snapped his head back staring ahead. Then without turning his face he put an arm out in Rosie's direction. She raced for him, climbing onto his knee and laying her head against his flannel she began to sob again.

"See! Father loves you, Rosie," Grace cried.

"Stop crying now Rosie!" said Letty.

Mother fixed her dull eyes on Grace and Letty. "You two finish your dinner," she said.

"What about Fred's dinner?" Letty asked, sitting down.

"Pass it up and I'll put it on the saucepan," Mother said.

"We'll put Tom's in the pig bucket," Grace said importantly.

"Tom might get bitten by a snake if he's hiding in the corn," said Letty.

Rosie lifted her face from Father's chest.

"Yes, a big black snake might bite bad Tom," she said.

Mother reached for Fred's dinner. She saw Father in a sideways glance. He stretched and snapped his head back at the sound of Tom's name. His swallow moved his red throat running down inside his flannel and turning brown at his chest.

His jaws snapped shut and his hard brown eyes darted at Tom's place.

He made a hissing noise under his tongue.

Mother had a vision of Tom flying through the green corn.

She blinked the dullness from her eyes.

One corner of her mouth twitched.

Mrs Halliday a heavy woman climbed the stairs to her
flat with her side to side walk, her shopping bag slung
over an arm as she used both hands to cling to the
banisters rather like someone climbing a rope.

Her stockings were falling down too, but she didn't
care. There was a cool dark peace on the stairs and in
the hallway and these were the times she felt she owned
102 Park Road.

But she wasn't alone as she thought. Reaching the
top of the stairs she saw a man and a woman standing
near her door.

The woman she knew. It was Josie Servani whose
flat was at the opposite end of the hall. Mrs Servani had
two daughters and was deserted by her husband. The
daughters were in school being ten and eight and the

family lived on a deserted wife's pension. Josie stood now with a hand crunched against her mouth and her eyes both frightened and laughing.

The man had a paper in his hand and with flared fingers made a crisp little edge to the fold.

"It's her," said Josie removing her hand and holding both prayer fashion to her lips.

"Mrs Rose Halliday?" said the man. She got the clear impression he was dismissing Josie who nevertheless removed her hands from her mouth and brought them together in a little clap.

The man frowned heavily.

"Inside?" he said to Mrs Halliday, holding out a hand palm upwards. He just about had his back to Josie.

Mrs Halliday unlocked the door, worried that she wasn't asking Josie in.

Immediately she was inside the lottery ticket sent to her by her son Tom for her sixty-fifth birthday appeared to spring at her from where it was propped against a coffee canister that held her rent receipts.

I'm being silly, Mrs Halliday said to herself turning from it and pulling out a chair for the man turning the cushion onto its better side.

But I know I'm not, thought Mrs Halliday creaking herself into a chair too and managing not to look into the man's face.

Josie was lingering not too far from Mrs Halliday's door when the man let himself out. On the second step

171

he paused and stared so hard at Josie with his chin tipped up she turned and scurried in the direction of her flat.

The man was seething. Sometimes on occasions similar to this he was given champagne, sometimes he was cried over, sometimes he was promised money (though this seldom eventuated) and mostly he was asked back for a celebration party (which he wasn't allowed to attend under a rule of the lottery office) but never had he encountered a winner like Mrs Halliday.

He remembered her at the table with her arms around her old shopping bag saying nothing.

A waste, a waste a waste! cried the man to himself getting into the car which was shabby and old and in need of replacing.

Give me a rich winner any time.

He got a swift mental picture of Josie, laughing with her head back, her fattish neck hung with pearls and that hand she held to her mouth ringed with winking stones.

"I can just see the bitch!" he said, his words drowned out with the roar of the engine as the car to his amazement started at the first attempt.

Inside her flat Mrs Halliday stared at the closed door as if daring it to open or be knocked upon.

She began almost noiselessly to unpack her shopping bag. First the meat. Unwrapping it a wave of happiness washed over her. She had asked for a piece for a stew and the butcher trimmed it ruthlessly, leaving pieces of red meat clinging to the fat he was discarding. He heard Mrs Halliday's intake of breath and flicking his eyes in her direction he put the handful of discards with the portion she was paying for.

"For your cat," he said wrapping it swiftly.

Mrs Halliday remembered his hands, so clean pale pink and smooth coming like a nice surprise at the end of his hairy arms.

"Such nice hands," she whispered putting the meat into the coldest part of the refrigerator.

She usually smelled it for freshness but felt this would be an insult.

She moved about as quietly as she could keeping an eye on the door. She couldn't remember it looking menacing before.

You look different, door.

Don't look different.

She sat at the table and tipped the contents of her purse out trying too late to stop the clatter.

She always counted her money after shopping.

But her hands hovered above it now and in the end she picked it up silently and put it back in the purse.

I don't want to make a noise, she said to herself.

Her eyes were on the door when there was a tap, one knuckle striking once almost shyly.

Mrs Halliday held her body in with her breath and didn't move.

It's not Josie, she told herself. Josie always gives the door one bang and shouts out "It's me!"

But she knew it was Josie.

I will say I was having a rest and didn't hear.

She got up without allowing the chair a squeak and went into the bedroom.

She got onto the bed the way she always did, kicking off her shoes and throwing her legs in the air, wriggling her bottom until it fitted into the centre of the bed. She blew strands of hair out of her eyes as she stared at the ceiling. She heard in her mind the tap of the door and tried to fit an expression to Josie's face.

I don't know how she was looking, she said to herself closing her eyes. But Josie's face kept floating before her and the doorknock repeating in her ears. She couldn't get comfortable and in the end sat up and pulled the covers back to look at the mattress. The pattern was gone, long melted into the thin dull grey fabric streaked here and there with rust. I should try and get that off worried Mrs Halliday. She rubbed a finger on a mark feeling a spring. She rubbed harder and the spring seemed on the point of bursting through the covering. She tried to lift a corner of the mattress thinking it was a long time since she had turned it over but the rolled edge was flattened with age and there was nothing to grip. She put the covers back and lay down again. But she couldn't rest. She put a hand underneath a buttock and rubbed again at the spot where the spring poked her. She moved like a hen settling into a nest and felt lumps around her thighs. Then she turned over and thought she smelled dust. It's old, she thought, older than Tom who was forty-five. I'll have to write and tell him. She wriggled and it was close to a writhe. I don't have to yet, she thought closing her eyes. A vision of Tom's wife rose before her. The wife's name was Mavis and she had sparse sandy hair and watery blue eyes without lashes and a nose that appeared to grow longer when she pulled her thin mouth in which she frequently did. Mrs Halliday turned away from the sight. She rubbed a leg against the mattress trying to smooth away a lump.

She appeared only to succeed in making larger lumps. It's just that I can't lie still, she said to herself. She willed herself to try but after a while gave up and sat up her hair in her eyes and both hands supporting her. A mirror was opposite and she looked long into it as if addressing another person.

"I will have a new one," she said and waited almost expecting it to answer.

"Yes, a new one," she said and lay back again. She imagined it richly coloured, smooth and firm and yielding gently to her body and smelling of newness.

She turned over and ran a hand down the side of the old one. I'll have to do something with you, she thought.

She judged the space under the bed but it would not fit there. She placed it with her eyes in different parts of the room but she saw it obscuring the window or making it impossible to open the door. Wherever it was it appeared to half fill the room with a bend in the middle like a drunken old woman struggling to stand upright.

That will be a problem, she thought.

Then she shot into an upright position again.

"Josie can have it!" she said aloud to the mirror daring it to argue.

She fished with her feet for her shoes beside the bed. Josie was forever talking about her need for a new mattress. She and one of the children slept on an old one bowed in the middle like the bottom half of a hoop. In the summer she packed spare blankets into the hollow and the bed when made up looked quite respectable.

Mrs Halliday raked her hair into some sort of order with her fingers and let herself out of her flat and hurried along to Josie's. She felt that fervent inner glow of someone about to do a good deed. The door was open and inside were the two girls leaning over the table where they took their meals and Josie had her back to the sink looking as if she had just imparted some news of great importance. She was startled when Mrs Halliday appeared and the girls drew back from the table as if attached to a length of string.

"Now behave yourselves both of you," Josie said to them pulling out a chair for Mrs Halliday. Josie turned to take cups from a shelf and set them on the table. The girls sat on one chair, one was a large child and the other thin. They wriggled their rumps together giggling.

"Behave, I said," said Josie sternly. "Behave in front of—" She lowered her eyes and set saucers under the cups.

I think she was going to call me Rose, Mrs Halliday said to herself astonished.

Josie addressed herself again to the girls.

"Remember you're only children!" she said.

They sobered while digesting this undeniable truth and pressed their chins to their chests allowing themselves a controlled titter now and again.

Mrs Halliday struggled in her mind to find something to say.

She thought of the meat but when the words started up she swallowed them back.

No, I won't tell her that, she said to herself averting her eyes so that she looked directly through the open doorway onto Josie's bed.

There was no build up of blankets in the middle and the dreadful sagging was emphasized because one of the children had obviously sat there when she came in from school. The head and foot seemed to bow towards each other but perhaps the pronounced dip gave this illusion.

Mrs Halliday saw not so much Josie's bed but her own.

She saw it as flat and smooth as a table top with the quilt on and not a lump or dip in sight.

Even staring into the cup of tea Josie placed near her elbow Mrs Halliday held onto the vision of her bed.

It's got years and years of wear in it yet, she told herself with a lifting of her spirits.

She lifted her cup too feeling Josie's watching eyes and waiting ears.

I'll have to say something or she'll wonder why I came, thought Mrs Halliday.

She broke the silence at last.

"What I really came for," said Mrs Halliday, "Was to ask you to give me a hand to turn my mattress over.

"There's no hurry," she said when Josie did not speak.

"Any old time will do."

The house was perched on the side of a hill with a verandah in front.

A few May bushes, one or two scraggy geraniums and a wild pink rose grew level with the verandah boards so the outlook to the road was unimpaired.

I had come home from school and found Mother on the verandah staring dreamily at the road. It was 1932 and a fairly steady stream of tramps went by but not many cars.

At school that day Sister Alfreda had seen a family on the road, a mother and father and three children. The mother and father walking together had packs on their backs and the spindly legged children were spread out with old rag hats pulled down to their eyes.

"A family on the road," said Sister, "God help them."

I looked at the picture on the classroom wall of Jesus with his fingers pointing to his bleeding heart, half expecting Him to step down and perform some miracle.

All the class rose like a flock of sparrows to crane through the window.

"Sit down!" Sister Alfreda said sharply. "You weren't told to stare like a herd of cattle!"

Mother did not watch the road for tramps.

She would leave whatever she was doing or when she was doing nothing and go out and look when she heard the noise of a motor that was not Creamy Ryan's lorry on its way to the butter factory or Father Slattery on his way to see some parishioner who hadn't been attending Mass regularly.

I had seen her snap Clem off her breast with the suddenness of a gun going off and fling him down roaring on the couch while she dashed out.

Now she was standing leaning against the verandah post, her eyes on the flat where a car was twinkling between the gums and the dog bush that lined the road.

The engine hummed with the noise of a droning bee, then took deep groaning breaths as it climbed the hill where the road had been cut through one side. I always wished the road was on our side of the hill. Then Mother could watch the cars for longer, and the dreamy shine would not fade so quickly from her eyes.

"I saw a woman in the front seat with a big black hat on," she said her voice just above a whisper. "There was a big pink rose under the brim."

How could she? It must have been that she was so tall with wonderful sight in her large blue eyes that made her see so well. I saw only a glint of sun on transparent side curtains, and a spare wheel at the rear almost hidden in a puff of blue smoke.

Mother wrapped her arms around the post as if it were someone she loved.

There was a crash in the kitchen. I knew by the sound one of the little boys had emptied the contents of the saucepan cupboard with the swipe of an arm.

"I'll see, Mother," I said.

In a little while she came down the hall into the kitchen so quietly I turned and found her. She mostly moved this way. In her spotty muslin dress she walked as I imagined a lithe mountain cat would. She stood staring at Eric aged three and Clem one and a half surrounded by pans on the floor. Eric stretched out an arm to her with his starfish fingers sprayed out. A little absent smile settled on her mouth then vanished when she looked at Clem standing up with a fly in the corner of his eye, one nostril running and only a singlet on.

"I'll get him some pants from the line," I said. Mother appearing not to hear me went to the stove, looked in the fire box then snapped the door shut. I had time to see a bed of ashes with one or two little pink points. She turned and leaned against a chair back looking over the kitchen table through the window into the peach tree. All over the table were the plates and cups from breakfast, the butter run to oil and the loaf of bread with the cut edge dry and curled like an old leaf.

"I'll get some wood for the stove," I said quite loud because I was never sure if she heard or not.

I went down the back steps to the little room that was both wash house and wood shed. Inside scattered about were several pairs of the boys' pants, most of them screwed into hard little lumpy heaps. A cloud of flies rose from a pair on the bottom of a dry wash tub. I found a bucket and put in all those I could see and poured on a flood of water. With a potstick I churned them round and round letting the muck rise to the top. Transferring the pants to a tub I flung the water deep into the May bush. Climbing on a stump of wood I balanced the old grey washboard against the tub and ground yellow soap into the stained parts of the pants, plunging them up and down in the fresh water.

I imagined myself saying to Mother, "I've washed all the boys' pants and hung them out, Mother," and seeing the smile chase the strain from her face.

In a little while a shadow fell across the tub.

"Oh Father!" I said, as if he'd frightened me. As if gladness could frighten you.

My blinking smile and his beautiful one washing into his brown eyes made nothing of the distance between us.

"Hullo Pinkie!" he said. "Little washerwoman Pinkie!"

He sat down in the doorway to unlace his old reddish boots caked with clay from the roadworks where he had a job. I had this urge to say something that would please him.

"Mother's not sick," I said to my red hands in the water. "She's getting tea."

He said nothing and I stole a look at his back, past the day's last piece of sun laying some gentle fingers on the edge of the tub. The back of his neck was creased beautifully like a doll's pleated skirt. When he moved the pleats deepened. His hair grew in and out of his collar touching him lovingly. His shoulders moved under his old blue shirt with the rhythmic unlacing. He made some nice little gentle grunts. My blouse felt too tight for my skinny chest, my throat too tight to swallow.

Beautiful Father.

"How was school today?" he asked with his last boot coming off.

"Oh, good," I said. "We saw a family of tramps. Sister Alfreda said to pray for them." I wrung at some old serge pants of Eric's. "I'm going to pray for them."

Father put his arms on his knees and let his hands hang down. Perhaps he hadn't heard.

"I saw a nest of robins," he said. "We didn't have to cut the tree down."

"Oh, I'm glad," I said.

After a while he said into the stillness: "I'll have to go inside soon."

"When I've washed the pants I'll come too," I said seeing his troubled face with the back of my head.

"Well Pinkie," he said stuffing his socks into his boots and standing up.

He went and I saw through the cut-out square above the tubs that evening had come. The clothesline stretched bleakly across the sky. The May bush was bent in the wind with the flowers parted like the hair of a white headed old woman. The road was quiet. No singing cars went by and there was no light in McTaggert's house on the other hill. The water in the tub, sloshy and lively before, grew still and chilly. I didn't want to wash any more. I took my arms out of the water and wiped them along the sides of my tunic and went to the bottom of the steps.

I heard Mother scream out: "Nancy said she was getting wood! It's not my fault the fire's out!"

The door opened and Father hurtled down the steps past me.

"You had to get wood for the stove!" he said.

"Oh Father I know!" I wailed.

184

Inside I saw the furniture had backed into the shadows taking Mother who was hard to pick out at first in the corner of the couch with both hands pressed flat against her face.

The little boys were staring at her in the shadows too except for their faces like pale discs.

With a moaning cry she dropped her head against the hard end of the couch and began to roll it from side to side.

Eric stood up with a scattering of pans and began to wail. A second later Clem started up so when Eric's wah—ahh—ahh—ah was dying away Clem's shrill scream cut across it. The three of them were like instruments of a human orchestra, someone was blowing unable to draw from them any sweet or hopeful sound.

Father was in the shed scrambling for wood that would burn quickly.

I had stopped on the middle step looking back and looking forward.

"Go inside!" he called to me.

Oh Father don't talk to me that way.

"Inside!" he said. "Clem's messed in a saucepan! The fire's dead out!"

I looked at him, nothing to see except the brown egg of his face tipped towards me. His mouth was jagged and ugly.

Oh Father you were so beautiful.

"Inside at once! Nancy! Get inside!"

185

Say Pinkie, Father. Please father, call me Pinkie. Oh Father, say Pinkie please.

He would not have heard the words if I had said them, for he was splitting wood with hard quick blows, sending pieces flying about. There was a wind too, one of those winds that come with evening, a wind with a breath of warmth from the day just gone and a chilly edge warning of worse to come.

Cheryl and Dennis saw the house with both sets of parents one Saturday morning.

They went early before the influx of people to the estate the young women in their weekend jeans and their young husbands straddling babies on their hips very often like the young Barkers with parents along.

The three women and Dennis went into one of the houses and the elder Barker and Adams, Cheryl's father, stayed near a bed of petunias at the base of a gum tree.

The salesman rushed to help the women up the steps to the porch which was unnecessary since the house was almost flat on the ground.

He looked expectantly towards Adams and Barker but their backs said clearly they would have no part in any inspection.

187

"All these places are the bloody same," Adams said licking the edge of his cigarette paper as he rolled a smoke.

"Gawd it's a long way out," said Barker.

They each thought with a sense of cosiness of their own places (rented) half a dozen doors from each other in Parramatta. They were semi-detached with the roof sloping down in Barker's case almost touching the dusty little hedge in front. Adams's place had the front verandah closed in as a bedroom for the Adams boy born when Mrs Adams was forty-three, ten years after the last of the three daughters.

Mrs Adams sat in her dark little kitchen and wept for most of her pregnancy. She hoped the child would be born dead or so severely handicapped it would go into an institution. When he was normal and a relative the same age as Mrs Adams bore a sub-normal child Mrs Adams became very proud of her achievement and spoiled the boy rotten.

The verandah room of faded canvas blinds did not enhance the Adamses' place because their neighbour kept the exposed front and the cottages had the appearance of a face with one eye closed.

Not that the Adamses or the Barkers noticed this kind of thing.

When the Adamses' lawn mower broke down once, it stayed in the middle of the tiny lawn for the remainder of the summer and the grass grew high enough to cover it.

The Barkers had an old canvas chair on their lawn with a split in the seat through which the grass grew. Barker never bothered to move it when he cut the grass, grumbling and cursing and throwing old shoes and dogs' bones that got in his way into the hedge.

Adams and Barker were always in a hurry to get to the club. The wives were the same.

Making sure she had her cigarettes and money for the poker machines Mrs Adams (Mrs Barker too) would bang the front door shut and pick her way down the steps where missing tiles gave them a gap toothed look and make for the club leaning forward as she walked as if this would bring it closer.

The two couples formed a foursome when Cheryl and Dennis married. The women took great pleasure in comparing notes on what the two families were up to in pre-marriage days.

"Fancy that!" Mrs Adams said when she learned the Barkers were also in a rented cottage at The Entrance for a holiday in January 1960.

Both swore they remembered Cheryl and Dennis making up to each other on the sand.

"She used to talk about this little boy," Mrs Adams said looking into her beer with eyes as moist.

Mrs Barker dreamily stroked her glass.

"I remember this little girl in red swimmers," she said.

"Gawd," said the men looking around to find the drink waiter again.

Cheryl and Dennis spent the first two years of their married life in a rented flat and were now ready for something better. Cheryl worked the switchboard of glass factory by day and Dennis drove a delivery van for a grocery warehouse. At night both worked in clubs and hotels serving at the bar, washing glasses and waiting on tables.

A place of their own was their dream. They had saved enough for a deposit and were now deciding between a block of land and building to a plan they liked ("Gawd they'd be findin' fault with it inside a year," said Adams or maybe it was Barker) or going into one of the places already built on estates like this one.

Adams and Barker showed little interest in either scheme beyond wondering how anyone could be bothered undertaking such a project

"I couldn't take that movin,'" Barker said over his Saturday beer.

"They'll be leavin' it to their kids to pay for," said Adams gloomily taking up his glass.

Cheryl and Dennis had no car because all their money went into their home savings account and the senior Barkers with a beaten up old Holden were prevailed upon to drive to the estate this Saturday. Barker agreed to go only if Adams went.

"Show an interest," said Mrs Adams with some severity. "It's the least you can do."

Mrs Barker had said the same earlier on to Barker who complained for the thousandth time in their married life that she was too bloody useless to get a driver's licence and if she had acquired one Adams and Barker might have been spared the trip.

They showed their reluctance to become involved in the exercise by keeping their backs to the little place Cheryl and Dennis and the mothers spent about twenty minutes inspecting.

A noise made them turn.

It was Mrs Adams swinging her handbag at them.

"Oh Gawd," said Adams and Barker.

"Come and look," she said.

"At what?" said Adams.

"The place!" said Mrs Adams.

"There's no room in there to swing a cat!" Barker said.

"Come *on*," Mrs Adams said.

"Gawd," said the men throwing their cigarettes into the petunias.

They followed Mrs Adams's back and trotting legs.

Cheryl and Dennis and Mrs Barker and the salesman were in a room that seemed all the house.

Behind one jutting counter was the kitchen and behind another a built-in table and seats.

"No dining room suite to buy," said Mrs Barker dreamily stroking the surface of the table.

The salesman gave his head a knowing little shake as if he had personally organized this.

Cheryl stood holding her elbows looking upwards as if she was seeing angels. She had her mouth open and her tongue wandering about as if trying to check her perpetual smile. She had washed her hair before leaving home and it hung like bootlaces around her whitish face. Her legs and feet in thongs were the same whitish colour. Her cotton dress was shapeless and dipped unevenly around her knees that looked like uncooked buns.

Dennis stood a little distance from her rubbing a forearm and running his eyes around the skirting board and window frames keeping them away from Cheryl as if too shy to show her the happiness in them.

"Great," he said.

"Oh, it's beautiful!" said Cheryl the last syllable engulfed in a sigh rising from her chest.

"Well you two?" said Mrs Barker looking at Adams and Barker who appeared almost to be clinging together just inside the doorway.

They began to feel in their hip pockets for smokes.

The salesman embraced Cheryl and Dennis and the mothers in a look of conspiracy.

"I'll be back in a minute," he said as Adams and Barker went closer together to give him room to get past them.

"Look at the rest of it," said Mrs Adams glaring at Adams and Barker.

They did not move but cast their eyes towards an opening into a small hallway as if to say this was seeing all.

"It's nearly dinner time," said Barker with a whining edge to his voice.

"He means gettin' to the club!" said Mrs Barker curling her lip and dumping her handbag heavily on the dining table.

Cheryl looked to see if it left a mark.

Mrs Adams reached down and smoothed around the edges of a cupboard and Cheryl watched as if she should perhaps censor this.

The salesman returned. He had two handfuls of printed and illustrated matter which Adams and Barker saw were bright and bold with pictures of houses and drawings of house plans. He put a handful into each of the hands of Mrs Adams and Mrs Barker.

"Gawd," whispered the men looking across at the car by the petunias and wondering when they could decently escape to it.

The salesman pressed past them grinning as if he had just won a major prize with Cheryl and Dennis following him looking only a shade less so.

"Don't wait for us, "said Dennis.

Adams and Barker and their wives halted in a little heap on the gravel path.

The salesman looked back leading the way to the little office on the estate.

"Well get them home safely," he said.

"Gawd," said Barker making for the car.

Silently they climbed in, the women in the back.

The car started off ripping at the gravel and discharging rudely from the rear. Safely away and on the highway Barker with one of his eternal cigarettes jutting upwards and looking in danger of setting a thick thatch of grey hair alight called to the back: "Youse all right back there?"

The women clutching their brochures each flung a head towards a window.

"Will we go 'ome first or straight to the club?" said Adams.

"We gotta boy at 'ome waitin' for his lunch!" shouted Mrs Adams. "He's forgot!" she muttered as if this did not surprise her.

"He's done for himself before!" said Adams.

"And he'll do for himself again if you got anything to do with it!" shouted Mrs Adams.

"Gawd," whispered Barker.

"Drop me at 'ome anyway!" said Mrs Adams and she would have flounced if her substantial rear had not been anchored to the rattling seat.

"What about you?" shouted Barker and it had to be taken for granted he was addressing his wife. He seldom if ever used her first name.

"'Ome for me too," said Mrs Barker.

"Gawd," whispered Adams.

They came upon the Adamses' place first so Barker pulled up and the two men sat without turning their heads. Mrs Adams was on the side nearest the kerb and she looked through the car window. She looked away almost at once.

"Gawd look at it," she said.

They looked though barely seeing the long straggling lawn, the opening between the edge of the blind and the verandah rail showing the top of a chest of drawers littered with bike parts, tattered magazines, empty drink cans, odd socks, a rubber surf vest and shorts that had been left to dry stiff with salt. The bowed end of the unmade bed was also visible.

Barker waited at the wheel and Adams turned and blinked his eyes on his wife.

"Git out or stay in," he said.

"I'm stayin' in," she said, "What does it look like?"

Mrs Barker fingering the brochures on her lap turned away to look out her window.

Barker turned and blinked at her.

"You can walk from 'ere," he said.

"I'm walkin' nowhere," said Mrs Barker.

"Gawd," said the men wondering what was next.

Barker decided. He started up the motor and turned the car around grazing the kerb on the other side and causing the women to hang onto the front seat and snap their legs together to save the brochures from littering the floor.

"He's headin' for the club!" said Mrs Barker.

"Where else?" said Mrs Adams.

"We'll be bloody lucky to get a parkin' spot," said Barker.

They found one and Adams and Barker got out with a show of briskness.

"If youse want to stay 'ere and wait youse can," Barker said.

"That's what they think!" said Mrs Barker scrambling out with Mrs Adams following.

Adams and Barker led the way faster than they usually did up a ramp that took them through swing doors into the club. A roar of sound met them but not a word distinguishable.

"Hardly a bloody seat left," said Barker.

But they found a table with a solitary drinker sitting sideways on his chair. They crushed around him and overwhelmed he swept his cigarette packet into his pocket and took up his drink and found a seat against a wall.

"Disruptin' everything gettin' 'ere late," said Barker.

They sat and the women laid their brochures on the table.

Adams and Barker avoided looking at them.

Thankfully the drink waiter was hovering not too far away.

"What do youse want?" said Barker and a second later he wished he had put it another way.

"We want a 'ouse," said Mrs Adams and Mrs Barker.

I dreamed there was a bear coming down the passage to my room.

Get up and close the door, I screamed to myself.

But I had that watery feeling in my limbs that dreamers have.

I screamed just as the blank doorway was about to be filled with the bear's shape.

When I woke it wasn't morning through the doorway, but a light from the kitchen.

There was still the noise of the bear's padding feet.

I sat up and screamed, "Mum!"

A low moan was the answer mixed with the rattle of a chair.

"Oh, shut up, shut up!" she said.

Then the chair creaked under another moan, and the padding feet started again.

Something was terribly wrong. I stared at the pale doorway wanting and not wanting to see her.

"Get up you and help me!" she cried. "Help me, damn you!"

I got out of bed and went to her.

She was on a chair, on the edge of a chair with her knees apart and her hands on them. I was struck by the whiteness and the newness of her nightgown. I stared at the blue flowers she had embroidered on the yoke and wondered why she hadn't taken care with something so pretty to fasten all the buttons at the neck. Her hair sprayed about and half covered her eyes but not the hate in them.

Two pin points of hate coloured grey blue.

"You do nothing to help me," she said.

She plucked at her kneecaps under her nightie. She was in the dining room called that because there was a dining table and chairs there, but we always ate in the kitchen. I looked through to the kitchen where a circle of the floor showed up from the hanging light bulb.

"I'll sweep the kitchen floor," I said.

"Oh, oh," she moaned in reply and her hair was flung about with the movement of her head.

She didn't want it swept then.

"Go and get Mrs Lister," she said, making circular movements on her thighs with her hands.

Mrs Lister.

She always said that red bitch up above.

I made for the door looking back at her not sure that she meant it.

"You don't want to help me, do you?" she said, rocking about.

The Listers' house was the next up the street from us, and was almost above us due to the steepness of the hill. Mrs Lister could stand at her window—and often did—and look down on our little back yard.

My mother would be there sometimes, pegging out clothes.

"Let the bitch stare," she said once flapping a towel free of creases before pegging it out in a slow deliberate way quite unlike her.

I was playing in the dirt that day making a little house out of dead wattle sticks with a roof of stiff dead gum leaves. Mrs Lister's breasts and thick red hair about filled the window. I had been so anxious before to get up to putting a little verandah on the house of sticks laid close together. But when I looked from Mrs Lister to my mother then back at the little house I didn't want to go on with it.

My mother hoisted the clothes prop jabbing it towards Mrs Lister who withdrew.

My mother laughed on her way back into the house.

But when I wandered into the kitchen she was on a chair crying.

I ran now out the rickety gate onto the street hoping some miracle would save me from asking Mrs Lister for help.

Albie Thomas was the miracle.

"Hey," he said when I opened the gate onto his skinny stomach. He was on his way home clinging to the fence because he was drunk.

"Mr Thomas," I said, "Mum wants me to get Mrs Lister."

The street light showed his surprise at me in my nightie. He put out a hand and pinched a piece of it over my tittie. He might have wanted to hold something to help him stand up. Then his hand strayed downward and I jumped back when it came to rest on my navel.

Mr Thomas let his hand fall and glanced up at Lister's house with a light in the back window. There were only a few other lights quite a way off, one outside the police station and another showing up the side way into the hotel. There did not seem to be help anywhere else but at Mrs Lister's.

Mr Thomas stared at my hand crunching the neck of my nightie. His eyes were watering a little, and his mouth was open a little and wet. His face had a shine on it like wet clay. I thought I might make Mr Thomas's head next time I played in the clay.

"Walk some of the way home with me. That's a better idea," he said. He put out a crooked finger and scratched at my waist. I looked up and saw the hairs in his nostrils.

"Mrs Lister!" I screamed.

Her window flew up.

"Mona!" Mr Thomas called.

"Get on home there, Albie," Mrs Lister called back.

She couldn't see me under the palings.

"Who sang out?" she said.

"Yu hearin' things, Mona," said Mr Thomas starting to walk off.

I stayed against the palings because Mr Thomas didn't want Mrs Lister to know about me.

There was a scream from our house and then I didn't care about Mr Thomas only Mum.

"Mrs Lister!" I screamed too. "Come to Mum!"

I heard her feet on her back steps and she ran through the stumps and old tins and tangle of weeds on the ground between our houses and over our side fence. I raced down the side of our place in time to see her land near our back door open and bright from the kitchen light.

She was like a lovely large white bird with a crest of red feathers. She was in a nightgown too, with blue ribbons tied under those big breasts which showed through the white nightie like the creamy underneath of a shell.

A little smile like a message of love was on her lips and in her eyes while she looked at me going up the steps.

A moan of my mother's hit us.

"Sarah!" Mrs Lister said. I did not know she knew my mother's name, let alone called her by it.

My mother now on a kitchen chair raised heavy dull eyes with hate in them for Mrs Lister. "You caused this," my mother said.

"That's not true now, Sarah," Mrs Lister said putting a hand on one hip and looking straight at my mother.

"It's true all right," my mother said, rocking about.

"Come on now, Sarah," said Mrs Lister with that little smile I wished was for me.

Mrs Lister looked at me. "Has she got a case packed, do you know honey?" she said.

Honey.

No one in the little town said honey only Mrs Lister.

She was saying it to me.

I went to the bedroom where the cases were and lifted a corner of the lid of one on top of a stack of three. Inside in beautiful array were white things I'd never seen before. There was a little nightgown on top embroidered with blue flowers the same as on my mother's new nightgown. I shut the lid, fastened the locks and hoisted it down.

My mother hated me with her eyes when I came into the kitchen with it. But Mrs Lister's eyes twinkled and crinkled all over me.

"Good on you, honey," she said taking the case from me and checking inside like I did.

"Now come on Sarah," Mrs Lister said, using the same words as before but meaning differently.

"I'm staying here," my mother said, sweat shining on her cheeks like Albie Thomas's. "Both of us can die."

"That wasn't what you thought at first now, was it Sarah?" Mrs Lister said with her little smile.

My mother reared back with a scream and Mrs Lister took her under the shoulders.

"Get away, get away!" my mother said but she yielded enough to take a couple of forward steps.

"You carry the case, honey," Mrs Lister said to me. I wondered if she knew my name was Clarice, and how wonderful it would be to hear her say it.

We made our way outside my mother walking like one of the ducks old Mrs Hadgett kept while Mrs Hadgett whom nearly everyone called nurse seemed to supply the women of the town with babies.

We got into the Listers' car in the shed beside the house and my mother clawed at the seat perhaps not wanting to be there. But Mrs Lister shut the door near her and got in behind the wheel with me in front. She looked back over her shoulder past my mother and her hands lay light as white moths on the wheel. My mother's stubby little red hands scratched at the seat back between Mrs Lister and me.

204

When I'm grown I'll drive a car like this, I thought. I'll wear a white gown threaded with blue ribbons and I'll drive through the night like this.

My mother moaned.

The car sped along by the river turning towards Hadgetts'. There was a screeching and squawking from the fowl yards when we got there and almost at once the hooped-over figure of Mr Hadgett came towards the gate.

There was light coming over the sky so if must have been getting close to morning. Mr Hadgett slept in a little shed near the fowls and ducks and they had probably wakened him. It was said in the town he preferred the noise they made to the crying of the babies. I was surprised to see him in clothes so early so it must be true that he never undressed at all.

He came up to the car, not seeing my mother or me only Mrs Lister.

"Mona," he said and wet his lips.

"Hullo Clive," Mrs Lister said turning her face and giving him that little smile. Mr Hadgett's eyes clung to her watering and blinking. The edges of his shirt cuffs under his coat showed a line of dirt like a pencil mark. Mrs Lister looked at them while his hands rested on the car door near me. He took his hands away and combed his sparse hair with his fingers.

"Who is it Dad?" Mrs Hadgett called from the verandah.

My mother moaned.

"Sarah Downs, Mother," Mr Hadgett said very quickly.

"I'll come," Mrs Hadgett said.

"I'll bring her up," Mr Hadgett said opening the back door, and taking my mother's case out. He moved fast for an old man.

Mrs Lister sat still and smiling until they moved clear of the car.

"Who brought her?" Mrs Hadgett called.

They did not reply, or if they did I didn't hear because Mrs Lister was turning the car around.

We sped away and I noticed Mrs Lister's beautiful waist with a soft bulge below like a baby's pillow.

"Put your head down honey and sleep if you want," she said.

She smelled of warm violets.

The sun was inside the car when I woke and we were outside the town near the camp set up by the old bridge. There was the start of a new one, ugly and raw looking, beside the old with its big willow at one end. It looked beautiful and solid and safe and I never could believe it was ready to fall down like the people said.

There seemed a lot of machinery about and a lot of men in the camp for just one bridge but I was glad my father had work. I saw him duck out of a tent and come towards the car looking and walking as if he couldn't believe what he saw.

He went around to Mrs Lister's side and laid one arm on the car roof while he looked down at her, sliding his eyes past her face to the blue ribbons tossed by the wind between her creamy breasts.

"I took Sarah in," Mrs Lister said.

"Is it here?" my father said.

"Probably," Mrs Lister said.

Half my father's face was showing below the edge of the hood. He wet his lips leaving his tongue showing between them. I saw the spit gathered around his teeth.

Mrs Lister put her tongue out too, wetting her parted lips. There was hardly room to see between their faces.

"I'll be in tonight," my father said, dropping his arm.

Mrs Lister bent down to move a gear stick and my father stepped back when the car started.

He stood in front smiling with his head back as if he defied her to run over him. She was smiling her smile through the windscreen at him.

A little way off the workmen were standing about the fire outside the tents where their breakfast was cooking. But they had their backs to it and looked hungrily down on us.

Mrs Lister put her head out the car window passing close by my father when he stepped aside.

"See you honey," she said.

The car gathered speed and the wind tore at her hair and the ribbons used all their frail strength to beat at her breasts and neck.

Her lips still shaped her smile but I fancied the wind carried this away too back to my father striding up to the camp.

I glimpsed him growing smaller and the men still like statues eyes fixed on him and mouths (I thought) half open.

Mrs Lister glanced down without any light in her eyes for me. They reminded me of the rock behind our place, pretty while the sun passed over it but blank when it was gone.

"Put your head down again honey, if you'd like another little sleep," she said.

I saw her body curved under the wheel like a white cloud. But I felt if I laid my head on it I would fall through into nothingness.

I looked away from her at the racing sky and the flying trees.

"I'll be all right, Mrs Lister," I said.

"You say Grammar. Why don't you say *Grandma*?"

Hetty Black said this to me in the ring of girls under the peppercorn tree at playtime in the grounds of St Joseph's Convent.

Tears rushed to my eyes. I plucked at some grass to hide them.

"She's crying," said Lilian O'Riordan.

"She bawls for nothing," Rose Boxali said, staring at me and putting a cheek almost on Hetty's shoulder to show what close friends they were.

Perhaps I imagined it but I thought they all edged a little away from me. I saw Sister Patricia at the bottom of the playground supervising the boys at football. When the ball flew up near her she put out a black laced-up shoe and sent it back. Then she straightened the crucifix in her belt and looked to see if Sister Francis who was in charge of St Joseph's had seen.

"Sister Patricia kicked the football," I said.

Everyone looked but it was far too late. Sister was just squinting against the sun, watching the boys.

"She didn't," Lilian said. "Now she's lying."

"She did before you looked," I said, misery making a mess of my voice.

"It's all right for a nun to kick a football," Rose said. "Isn't it Hetty?"

"It is if she wants to. But Sister Patricia didn't kick the football." Hetty fixed such fierce eyes on me I began to think I might have imagined it.

"We could tell Sister Francis that Nellie Wright said Sister Patricia kicked the football when she didn't," said Lilian.

"We could say that Nellie Wright says Grammar, and she should say Grandma," said Rose.

I looked away from them with an ache starting to come up into my neck with the effort of holding off from crying. The girls in the lower classes skipped on the bare patch of ground between the school and the gate leading into the convent where the nuns lived. Their hair bounced on their shoulders (Elsie MacMahon had curls like yellow sausages) and their tunics bounced on their knees. They skipped frantically inside the long rope held by Aileen Boyd and Stella Logan as if to ward off the clang of the bell when the playbreak was over.

210

Sister Francis came through the gate back to school after her eleven o'clock in the convent.

"There's Ssta now," said Rose. They said Sister like that, hissing it out between teeth and tongue.

Rose looked at Hetty and then at me. Rose's eyes said the time might be right to tell Sister Francis on me. I thought of praying but in the matter of Sister Patricia and the football it was like praying against a nun and God wouldn't approve of that. He might also expect me to say Grandma, not Grammar.

I plucked a blade of grass and chewed the sweet white end.

"You're eating grass," said Lilian.

"The Wrights are so poor they have to eat grass," said Rose, safely cuddled against Hetty.

"Why is your *Grandma*," Hetty pronounced it carefully, "housework mad? She never stops scratching like an old hen, my mother says."

"Yes," said Lexie Connolly whose farm was next to ours and who was wisest of all on the peculiar habits of the Wrights. "Before they finish eating she's into the washing up. We sit over our dinner table for hours and *hours*."

"So do we," Rose said. "Anyway cleaning and cleaning doesn't make any difference to the Wrights' old place."

"We're clean," said Lilian. "But not mad clean, like old Mrs Wright."

Rose whispered into Hetty's ear. It was about me because both pairs of eyes were on me during the whisper. Then Rose drew back. "Your brother Bernard is mad," she said.

A couple of the girls breathed "oooh" at this daring but as Hetty and Rose and Lilian were the power at St Joseph's they just dropped their eyes and plucked at the grass.

Sister Francis now inside the classroom threw up a window.

"Two girls please to put the desks back for singing," she called.

The ring of girls flung their arms in the air. "Me, Sssta. Me Ssta. Please Sssta, Sssta," they cried.

"Mary Caldwell and Alice Lawler," said Sister Francis shutting the window.

"Poke your tongue out at them," said Hetty when Mary and Alice could be seen through the window moving desks and seats.

Thank you God, I thought. If Hetty or Rose or Lilian had been called they would almost certainly have taken the opportunity of telling on me. In my relief I plucked more grass and began to chew it very hard.

"She's eating grass *again*," said Rose.

Why do you call your brother Bernard, anyway?" said Lilian. "Everyone says Bernie."

The grass danced under my eyes, but there was no wind stirring it. Bernard danced there too. I saw him on the kitchen couch with his roley poley body and his great round head that bounced and shook almost without stopping. I hated him with all my heart.

"Yes," said Rose "There's Bernie O'Reilly and Bernie Caldwell.

"No one calls them Bernard."

"Grammar and Bernard," mocked Hetty.

I looked over the school ground at Patterson's corn paddock and the creek where a string of cows stumbled through a water hole on their way to the other bank. Everything swam because of the tears. How do I stop? Our Father who art in heaven. Don't let me cry. Mother of God help me. There was loneliness everywhere. Patterson's house was on the hill with the windows shut and no smoke coming from the chimney. The Pattersons got up at four o'clock in the morning, an hour before the other farmers and went to bed after the milking. They got up then to go to the yard at two o'clock in the afternoon. There was a story about Mr Patterson in his nightshirt and Mrs Patterson in a flannelette nightgown chasing a man selling saucepans who banged on their door at twelve o'clock in the day. They were so wild they chased him through the school grounds and the nuns blessed themselves and turned their backs at the language and the sight. People were risking Patterson's curse if they called at the farm in the middle of the day, the town said.

In the bottom corner of the playground were the lavatories. They sat there snug with the long grass on three sides of them. They did not wink cold bossy eyes like the windows of the school. I could go there and sit on the scrubbed pine seat and cry myself out. Then I could wash my face pretending to get a drink of water and hang around the taps until it was time to go in. I got up and ran.

"Ooh. Aah..." I heard Rose say, "She's going to the lavatory and it's bell time!"

The bell did peal out when I was bolting the door.

Stop crying now, I told myself laying my face on the grey walls of the lavatory in the luxury of being alone. Holy Mother, stop me. The bell clanged with an urgency that said woe betide those who disobeyed it. That set me crying harder.

I would never stop now in time to run and join the straggling end of the lines. But I'll stop soon, I thought. Soon I'll stop. Think of something good, something funny. Think of someone. Pa, Ma, Grammar. Why do we say Grammar? Who started it? I hate them all, I thought. I hate every one of them. Down against the wood ran my tears. Singing would be started. Sister Patricia bent over the piano would be striking notes with her long white hands in her long black sleeves. If anyone played up she saw them reflected in the glossy wood of the piano. For a long time I believed her when she said she had eyes in the back of her head (was that

214

counted as a lie?). I pictured the half circle of children ready for "Nymphs and Shepherds". None of them liked me. None of them put their arms around me at playtime.

If Hetty and Rose and Lilian left St Joseph's would it be different then?

Hetty and Rose and Lilian.

A picture of them shot across my mind with arms flung in the air.

"Ssta, Sssta, Nellie Wright went to the lavatory when the bell was going. Can we go and get her? Sssta, Ssta?"

Come away, said the song. Come, come away.

Who would go away from St Joseph's? Half way through the school day? It was as daring as the Pattersons' chasing the saucepan man. I sneaked the lavatory door open.

The singing floated across the school ground.

Come away. Come, come away.

Yes. I will, I will! Before the porch door opens and Hetty Rose or Lillian come tearing towards the lavatory and me.

I plunged through the long grass to the fence, over it and down to the creek. Only one of the Pattersons' cows saw me, a black nostrilled placid old milker who tossed her head sideways as if to say she wasn't going to get out of my way.

You hate me too, don't you old cow Patterson?

I started crying again and running fast up the creek, almost dry because of the long spell without rain. I was going home the creek way! It was forbidden by Pa and Ma and Grammar because of the jagged rocks you had to leap across, the torrent of water when it rained in the mountain, the cattle straying there to drink, snakes, a man kangaroo at times.

As well there were boots chipped of leather on the rocks and sodden by the mud and slime. It was a sin as deadly as any recited from the catechism to go the creek way to and from school although it cut half a mile off the walk. "You go the creek way and you'll be skinned alive," Ma said a hundred times.

Walking was not that much easier the road way. The road was a series of ruts and bumps and the few cars belonging to the farms on our side of the town travelled over it at a snail's pace. We sometimes got a lift. You couldn't tell whether the cars were going to stop or not, so you tried to look as if it didn't matter. Once I saw the Clem Murphys coming and knew they wouldn't give me a lift because Mr Murphy and Pa were fighting about a dividing fence that was falling down and Pa didn't want to do his share of the repairs. I was surprised when they slowed down almost to a dead stop, and as I was about to step onto the running board, the car leapt forward and I fell back into the tussocks. Clem and his son Tiny (Pa said Tiny was madder than Bernard) roared with laughter looking back at me while they bumped about in the front seat.

I wept anew at the memory, dragging sobs from my chest paining with the effort of running.

I suddenly felt something different about my right arm. It had a feeling of emptiness. I knew. I'd left my school bag behind hanging in the porch with the others. I pictured it there in isolation at dinner time and Hetty or Rose or Lilian snatching it up and pulling out my beetroot sandwiches.

"Look, she's got beetroot sandwiches," one of them would say. "Beetroot! It always runs into the bread. Ugh! We *never* have beetroot sandwiches."

I saw them running to the circle of children holding my shameful sandwiches aloft for all to see, offering them around, but no one accepting food from the poor Wrights' kitchen. I wept and sniffed, sobbed and ran, jumping from rock to rock and landing sometimes on the edge of a waterhole, surveying soaked boots with soaked and stinging eyes. I ran as if I was being chased, wondering why I did because I would arrive home hours ahead of the usual time, and Pa and Ma and Grammar would want to know why.

I teetered on the edge of a sheet of rock that fell away into a narrow gully, sloping up the other side. You needed to leap across the gully, landing half way up the slope to scramble to the top. I wiped my eyes on my tunic hem to get ready for the jump.

Then stopped.

Across the slope lay a snake, a long shining soft and slippery snake taking the midday sun.

It reminded me of a thick brown line nicely curved drawn on the blackboard by Sister Francis under words for spelling. The line moved showing an underneath creamy pink like a strawberry flavoured custard I'd seen once on the convent table. A deadly red bellied snake! The shock stopped my crying, and I heard a noise that was my breath drawn upwards from my ribs. The snake heard too. It raised its head and flashed out a forked tongue.

This is my side, said the eyes above the straight little mouth.

Come across here and see what happens.

I saw the creek wind on behind it, remote as another world. Perhaps I was to stand there forever, frozen into a still shape. I began to whimper with a hand across my mouth.

"Shoo," I said. "Go away! I'll poke you with a stick!" The snake did not move and neither did I because our eyes were rivetted together. I started to sob.

"I've got a gun in my bag back at school to shoot you!" I cried. Holy Mother, I lied. It was a bad time to lie. Our Father who art in heaven. Go away. Go away! It raised its head a little more. Now it looked like a badly drawn question mark. I stood not crying now, just breathing in and out. I moved. My boots caused it. The iron clips put on the soles by Pa to make them last slipped and scraped the rock. Oh my God, don't let me fall! Don't let me slide down the slope with the snake coming down on top of me, the two of us tangled together. I screamed at the thought, and the snake as if the sound came to it from a long way off, put its head down calmly and with a beautiful grace, began to half slither half roll, down the slope towards the bottom.

I screamed again. "It's coming after me!"

But at the bottom it pulled itself along, barely rippling its back, moving smoothly and swiftly towards the bushes on the bank. I heard a gentle whispering rustle; I saw its tail barely flick and it was gone.

The stillness lasted only a second without a little sound breaking it. "It's back!" I yelled.

But it was only a small brown bird landing on the twig of a tea tree and it fluttered off in fright. I stood holding onto the quiet too afraid yet to jump where the snake had been. Then from somewhere up the creek came a bellow. A bull! Patterson's bull! A great sturdy fellow with a neck as wide as a chimney and ferocious horns. I was saved from a snake but a bull would gore me to death! Holy Mother help me. Our Father which art in heaven. You don't say which! The Protestants say which! Say who. If Hetty Black heard me! I began to weep again with a shrill squealing noise I hadn't made so far. It did not drown out the bull's roar. Was it coming closer, or was it my fancy? The sound seemed just around the next bend of the creek and I imagined the bull breaking out of the saplings and charging at me with its head down ready to toss me high in the air then stab me with its horns while I rolled under the shadow of its great chest.

Was I going to die today? Holy Mother, would I be in heaven before nightfall? No, no. Please no! Pa, Grammar, help me! I turned and fled towards the creek bank, the one opposite to the direction the snake took, and closest to the road. I would have to take the road now for the last mile, at the mercy of the Motbeys or the Cullens or the Whitbys who might be getting home in time for the afternoon milking. They would offer me a lift to find out what I was up to. Then when their young came home from school the kitchens would be filled with the buzz of tongues.

Nellie Wright went home from school at eleven o'clock without telling Ssta! It would take a lot of bucket rattling by fathers and big brothers to get them outside to help at the dairy with news like that to chew over with bread and melon jam!

I plunged ahead running on the road only when the bush beside it was impassable. When I heard a noise I imagined was a car or sulky I fled for a gully. It was a miracle my tunic wasn't torn to shreds because I was stabbed with dead stalks of ferns and scratched with blackberries. But I ran and wept, stumbled, sniffed and cried, heaved and sobbed. Sometimes away from the road and unable to see it because the fence was bent over and hidden by tussocks I would stand and scream, "I'm lost! I'm lost!"

But I wasn't. Cawley's old place, long abandoned since they built a new house on the hill, told me I had two more bends to round before I was in sight of home. Tears of relief ran down my face and I sniffed at them trotting along the road now.

Then it came into view. Our place. It was on a little fat hill close to the road and looked like a face with a hat drawn down over its eyes. I stared and cried some more. It seemed to be all roof with no fence or trees to hide its shameful smallness.

"Your house looks like Humpty Dumpty on a wall," Rose had said once, and all the girls had laughed because it was true.

There was no gate or ramp leading to it, just rough steps cut into the clay bank by Pa, and now worn so much they ran into each other, so that you slipped and clawed your way to the top. Why did we have to live here? Why were we so poor? I think I'll walk past. I'll walk on and on to the top of the mountain and down the other side. I'll walk till I fall down and die. I wept some more.

Then level with the house I looked up and on top of the bank where other people would have a garden were Pa and Ma, Grammar, Bernard and Arnold lined up and staring down at me.

"It is our Nellie!" Arnold said.

"Was there a half holidee?" Grammar asked.

"That damn clock's slow," Ma said glancing back at the farm as if she expected to see the cows streaming home as they sometimes did around three o'clock.

"Slow be damned!" Pa said. "That clocks runs like a waterfull since I gave it that good oiling."

"Trouble is you can't see the numbers on the face for the oil," Arnold said.

"You're right, Arnie," Ma said with a laugh like a fox's bark.

Arnie not Arnold, but Bernard not Bernie. Of course. Hetty and Rose and Lilian and all the world knew he was different.

I looked up at him. The sun was behind his head which seemed larger than ever, like a great round pumpkin I saw once caught on a fence post and hanging by its slender vine, wobbling away there and refusing to fall.

I felt a fresh rush of tears.

"She's crying," Grammar said hopping like a small grey bird to the edge of the bank. "Help me help her up, one of youse."

"Arnie," Pa said, "You and me'll have to put some logs in here and make some proper steps 'fore too long. I know just the tree for it."

Ma gave her little bark again. "That tree needn't worry about losing its head. It's safe I reckon for another twenty years!"

"Come on girl," Grammar said, pulling me up.

"Look at the scratches on her legs," Arnold said, "Who took to you with a briar stick?"

Leaning against Grammar's skirt I sobbed out, "Hetty Black and them!"

"The varmints!" Ma cried, "Hear that, Pa? You go straight to that nunnery after milking and give them a tongue lashing. Getting around dangling those beads and not looking sideways because of those fool hoods! They see nothing! Hear me, Pa?"

Ma was the only one in the family not really a Catholic.

"Let's git to the bottom of it," Pa said. "Did you say something to Hetty Black to rile her, girl?"

"I said nothing, Pa. Nothing at all!" I cried, fists burrowed into my eyes as we crossed the verandah and went through the front room into the kitchen.

"Hetty Black!" Ma said with scorn. "Ask her has she seen her birth certificate, and her Ma and Pa's marriage certificate. Ask her which one came first."

"You'd never find either of them in Nora Black's dresser drawers," Grammar said, "She hasn't cleaned them out since Hetty was in napkins."

"Always shitty too," Ma said.

"Never mind the Blacks," Pa said, "Sit the girl by the stove there. Has she had any dinner?"

Tears flowed again with the pangs of hunger tearing at my insides. The remains of midday dinner were still on the table.

"Snakes alive!" Grammar said wildly snatching at cups and plates. "We been out there staring at the road wondering what was coming, and the washing up not started!"

"Where's your school bag?" Ma asked staring at my legs, around which it usually hung.

I wept louder.

"I went to the lavatory and then came home," I sobbed.

"Didn't you get your bag?" Ma said, "Where's your beetroot sandwiches?"

"Hetty Black came after me with this big stick," I cried.

"Couldn't you've gone back for your bag?" Ma said. "You should've got your bag."

"Give her something to eat then," Pa said, "Cut her a slice of bread."

Ma held onto the loaf before it was swept into the tin by Grammar. She cut off an uneven slice. "It riles me to the core to think of them wasted beetroot sandwiches," she said.

"Have 'em tomorrow," Arnold said. At the thought I began to sob.

"Now stop bawling," Pa said, feeling along the shelf for his tobacco. "You gotta stop sometime."

Grammar was making a great clatter with the tin dish full of crockery and her red hands rubbing soap into a soaked and steaming dish cloth. Ma put the slice of bread on the edge of the table for me. I chewed on it with only a few tears running into the rancid butter.

Pa made his smoke. He wet the edge of the paper and curled it into a neat and slender roll. He was proud of it.

"Look at that one," he said to Arnold. "A machine couldn't turn it out better."

"When are you going to let me have a smoke, Pa? Arnold said. "I could roll a good one, too."

"You'll be rollin' no smoke in this house," Ma said. "Git out now and bring an armful of wood for the stove."

Pa pinched some stray tobacco from the end of his smoke. "I might take the axe before milking and knock a few stumps in around them fence posts in the calf paddock," he said. "They need straightenin' up."

"Look out for that brown hen if you're down that way," Ma said.

"If she's let a fox git her I'll kick her all the way to Brown Mountain and back."

Arnold brought the wood and dropped it heavily into the wood box.

"Start the milking without me, Arnie!" Grammar said. "I've got to give Bernard his wash and sew some buttons on his clean shirt 'fore I dress him."

On the couch Bernard wagged his head violently.

I stared into the stove. They had forgotten me already. I suffered because of them and they had forgotten me. Tomorrow would come and the cane from Sister Francis, and Hetty and Rose and Lilian under the pepper tree and me praying for the bell to go. Holy Mother, make it ring before they sày anything more. Holy Mother, don't let me cry. Tears began to run again.

"Stop bawling!" Pa said. "I said to stop bawling!"

I drew both hands down my sodden face. "A snake nearly bit me and Patterson's bull nearly got me!" I burst out.

They all stopped frozen still and open mouthed.

"Hear that!" Ma said. "She went the creek way!"

"That's how she got them scratched legs!" Grammar said.

"It wasn't Hetty Black at all. Haw, haw!" Arnold said.

"Well, I'll be damned," Pa said.

"'Hetty Black hit me with a briar stick'," Grammar mocked. "As if them nuns would let her!"

"A pack o' lies!" Ma said. "Is that all them nuns can teach her?"

"Hetty Black's growin' into a nice little thing," Grammar said.

"She always says 'Hullo, Mrs Wright' when she sees me at Mass."

"Goin' the creek way!" Ma said, as if she still couldn't believe it.

"Leavin' school halfway through the day. She'll catch it tomorrow!" Grammar said.

"She'll catch it today," Pa said. "She'll git a beltin' she won't forget in a hurry."

"Well give her one then," Ma said.

Pa said nothing.

"Git on with it!" Ma said. "Standin' there puffin' on a rotten cigarette. Wallop her now."

Pa smoked with his head down.

"Look at him!" Ma said. "All talk and no acshun as usual! She went the creek way and near ruined them good shoes. Look at them!"

All eyes were on my dangling legs and the scarred boots.

"Get off that chair at once and go with Arnie and help him put that separator together!" Pa said.

"'Yes, Pa,'" I said leaping off the chair.

"'Yes, Pa,'" Ma mocked. "Where's the wallopin' she was supposed to git?"

"You give it to her," Pa said.

"Listen to him! 'You give it to her.' He palms every job off he can on me. Hell soon be doin' nothin' but walkin' around rollin' cigarettes."

"Go on!" Pa said to me.

I went. I flew into the bedroom and peeled off my tunic and my boots and got into an old torn cambric dress. I went out the front way to avoid passing through the kitchen. Running past the window I heard Grammar

227

cackle. "She's going all right! She's runnin' faster 'an a stuck emu!"

Arnold was ahead. He slowed his pace and taking a stone bent sideways and threw it at a hen scratching in the beetroot patch. The stone spun cleanly, beautifully and the hen squawked and fluttered, racing away with wings almost level with the ground.

Alongside Arnold I took hold of the pocket of his old alpaca jacket. Over the dairy roof the sky was pink as if someone had spread it with apricot jam.

I sniffed. A dry sniff. My face was stiff. But dry. My eyes were cold around the edges. But dry.

"You stopped bawling?" Arnold said.

I had. It seemed years since I started but I had stopped last.

Pa was right.

You've got to stop sometime.

There was just enough light in the bedroom for Ted to pick Joan out over the foot of his bed.

She had on her old slacks and pullover and with her head tipped to one side was brushing her long grey and blonde hair as if she couldn't wait to have done with it.

Ted snapped on the light at his bedhead. His round eyes in his round head sitting in a blue pyjama collar showed briefly before he snapped the light off and slipped down on his pillow again.

Joan began to pull the clothes from her bed.

"You needn't get up right away," she said.

"Shut the door when you go out and I'll stay here for the rest of the day," he said.

She smacked a pillow as if it were someone's bottom.

"Oh Ted," she said.

"Stop saying 'oh Ted.' Start saying 'hey, you.' That's what I am when they're around."

"Oh Ted," she said again before she could stop herself.

There was a little more light in the room when the bed was made showing the outline of Ted, humped a little forward staring ahead. Joan sat on a chair, hands between her knees.

"Who's coming?" said Ted. He took his pipe from an ashtray near the bed and knocked it on the side of the table. Joan didn't actually wince, just breathed in a little sharply.

"Everyone," she said.

Ted sucked on the lighted pipe. "I see. Everyone."

"Oh Ted. You know what I mean."

"Yes Joan, I know who everyone is."

"I just meant all the children are coming," she said, slightly wistful.

She got up to take some clothes from the chair back and hang them in the wardrobes.

"Lois too," she said.

"You said everyone," Ted said, quite sharp.

"Ferdinand will be along," said Ted after a pause in a needling voice.

"Of course. And call him Phillip. That's his name."

"Ferdinand. Full of bull," said Ted.

"Annie's man. Your daughter Annie's man. Gentle and kind and honest. A good father, Ted." The tremor in her voice was barely audible.

"They've got you well tutored, Joan."

She took a jacket and a brush to the window and rubbed at the collar by the better light. "Are you going to do some things for me like giving the paths a good sweep?" she said in an amiable voice.

Ted didn't seem to hear.

"One of the great pleasures of my life once was to talk about my kids. One by one I've had to drop them as subjects."

"You've made the choice," said Joan.

"I'll never forget that day at the depot when I was telling Wally about Annie. I'd told him about Annie topping the secretarial class at college and now she had this great job. That night when I got home you brought out the brandy bottle and said 'Drink this while I tell you about Annie. She's three months gone and she doesn't want to see the father any more. She's keeping the baby.'" He ran a thumb around the cold bow of his pipe. "Wally still asks me how's Annie going in that great job of hers."

"That's a long time ago now Ted."

"Yes. Four kids ago."

Joan swung the jacket on a hanger and jabbed it on the wardrobe rail. "You repeat that story over and over. You know when Annie went to live with Phillip

231

she chose to have her second baby. She had this terrible guilt complex because the first was an accident. She's a wonderful girl, Ted. Look how she took Phillip's two, loving and caring for them when their own mother walked out on them."

"Swam out on them."

"Oh, Ted." Joan shut the wardrobe door with a snap. "Stop harping about that boat. Some people like living on a boat."

"Remember Clive and June Harris? I picked this fare up the other day and it turned out to be Clive. We only had Annie when we knew them, remember? He asked about Annie and I said she was married. I couldn't say my daughter had four kids and wasn't married. Clive asked me where she lived and I said 'Gunnumatta Bay.' He was impressed. He said 'Close to the water?' and I said 'Couldn't be closer mate. In fact she's right on top of it.'"

Joan sat on the chair again. "So they're not married. What's a slip of paper?"

Ted's voice was sad. "Joan, you're starting to talk like them."

"I do talk to them, Ted."

"I can't talk to Ferdinand. I was away sick the day they had Italian at school."

"You were in Italy during the war. And you look on Phillip as if he came from Mars."

"I was in Italy fighting against Ferdinand's relatives in the war."

"I always thought they were on our side," Joan said.

Ted put his pipe on the tray. "Every day you get farther and farther away from me, Joan."

She got up and raised the blind a few inches. "Your old war's got nothing to do with Phillip. He's a nice boy if you would try and get to know him. Look how he loves little Kerry."

"Which one's little Kerry?"

"You're being silly and insulting. Your first grandchild. Phillip loves her like his own. Try and remember there's a lot of love in that little house."

"Boat."

"All right then, boat!" Joan looked at her feet, hands between her knees again.

"Joan!" Ted said so suddenly she jumped. "Let's get away from it all." She looked at him but his eyes were on the doorway as if he was planning soon to pass through it.

"Do you remember how I wanted to do something different when we were young?" he said.

"I remember. You wanted to buy a fishing boat and we were supposed to live in a tent on the banks of the Hawkesbury. Then you wanted to go to Lightning Ridge and dig for opals.

"We were supposed to live in a galvanized iron tank turned upside down. Or sideways. I just forget."

233

"We nearly made it too. Only you said 'I'm pregnant again. Isn't it wonderful?'"

"So it was. It made four, two boys and two girls. Think of all the people who dream of having the perfect family."

"My advice to them is to keep it a dream."

Joan's voice was wistful. "I wish you wouldn't talk that way."

Ted put a short arm towards her with a stubby hand at the end. "If you really love me Joan come away with me. We could buy a little run down motel on the coast and do it up. We'd get a good price for the house and the taxi. We could work together, be together all the time. The two of us like it was in the beginning." He started off quite casual, then had to curb his eagerness.

"I'd love it, Ted," she said dreamily.

"Then what are we waiting for?" He sat up straight as if he would start moving that instant.

"No, we can't go just yet."

"No," Ted, body and voice sinking down as if it were the bed that anchored him. "You'll never leave them, Joan."

Joan turned her toes in and leaned forward, young looking except for her worried face. "I would if they didn't need us. But just take Annie. They're saving for a house. Annie's got to work for a while. Who else would mind the children?"

Anger took charge of Ted's voice. "Yes, who else? Who else would turn our happy home into a kindergarten. Nearly every day in the week, one of Annie's, two of Ferdinand's and one of Jerry's. I used to love calling in for a cup of tea when I had a fare out this way. Now it's like arriving behind the Pied Piper. I don't come any more. You probably haven't noticed."

She had, so she was silent.

Pleading replaced Ted's anger. "Come away with me, Joan." he said. "Let's tell them today we are going to sell out and go north. Too far away for them to find us. They don't have cars because they say cars pollute the air. They couldn't walk. Think of the condition of Tim's feet if they walked."

She smiled to tell him she believed he was joking. "Tim likes to go barefoot. Lots of young people don't wear shoes all the time these days."

"He's another one I don't talk about any more. Wally is always saying to me 'Where is Tim teaching now?' I never told Wally Tim gave up teaching to live in a hole in the wall. I never told Wally Tim wears one earring and a skirt and lives on seaweed and herbal tea."

"Ted! Just because Tim wore a caftan here once."

"And I looked at him and thought 'I couldn't introduce him to my best mate as my son.' I can just see the look on Wally's face."

"Tim's an artist. You should be proud."

Ted didn't snort but it was as if he had.

After a moment Joan said, "I should be out there in the kitchen doing things." But she didn't go.

"Don't do them," Ted said. "Come out for the day with me. Let them make their own lunch. We could go to a Sunday movie. Or we could sit by the harbour and talk about going away together. Why can't we?"

"Because we can't, Ted. Of course we can't."

"Of course we can't," Ted said in such a voice Joan got up and went to the dressing table and pulled the pins out of her hair.

"You've done your hair," Ted said.

"I know," Joan said.

He couldn't see her face, only her body crooked with the effort of brushing and pinning.

"Leave your hair down," Ted said. "I just got a whiff of it. Honeysuckle. Come to bed with me."

"Oh Ted," she said with a crooked smile.

Their eyes met in the mirror. But she saw also the custards to be made for the babies, the steaks to be seasoned (leaving one without garlic for Tim), the table to be set, the vacuum run over the floors. It blotted out everything including Ted.

"I wish there was time," she said.

"But there isn't," he said.

She sat on the bed near his legs and noticed how swiftly he moved them. She looked with envy at the legs of the dressing table. Oh, lucky things. Nothing to do but hold up a set of drawers with claw feet sunk deep into the carpet.

"Come on," he said putting his legs back and moving one against her rump. "I need something to bolster me for the ordeal ahead."

She jumped as if she'd been hit.

"Don't!" she said.

"Don't what?"

"Talk that way. I don't like it."

He stared at the quilt between his feet and Joan stole a look at his face.

She said gently, "It's OK for us to talk about selling out and going away. Something for the future. To talk about at least."

"Stop talking to me as if I was Jerry's little Bramble." Ted said.

"Bramwell."

"Even the names they give their kids are an embarrassment to me. To say nothing of Jerry."

She was silent.

"The last family day we had, Jerry told us he was chucking up engineering to take on glass blowing. Jerry was the one I talked about the longest. To steer Wally away from the others I talked about Jerry. I put a boy through University. I could say I had an engineer for a son. But what does Jerry do? With a house not half paid for he says 'I don't wanna be an engineer. I wanna be a glassblower.'"

"If Jerry wants to blow glass and he's happy blowing glass we have to go along with it."

"Those words have an ominous sound," Ted said.

"What's ominous about Jerry blowing glass?"

"Going along with it is the ominous part. We had to go along with it when Annie got accidently pregnant and when she got intentionally pregnant. We had to go along with it when Tim gave away teaching for bludging, and we have to go along with it when Jerry throws up everything he's worked for and we've worked for to blow something he says is a fruit bowl but looks to be more like a deformed pear. It all boils down to one thing."

Joan looked at the scuffed toes of her shoes.

"Hand outs from us," Ted said, "Money. Cash. The stuff they despise. They don't even say the word. They get you to. 'Ted, can you spare fifty? Ferdinand's got toothache and the dentist charges. Annie can't keep a goat on the boat. She's got to buy milk.'"

She smiled the smile that said she liked him joking.

"What's Jerry and his wife and kids going to live on until he blows the right shaped glass?" Ted said, "Tell me that."

Joan stood up. "Oh Ted, I've got enough on my mind and so much to do. Get up and give me a hand. Please, Ted."

He reached out and took her elbow. "Come to bed and give me your body. Please Joan."

She saw his reflection in the mirror. His round eyes in his round head jutted forward. He reminded her of a bulldog in a dog's home whom no one wanted. She smiled and he smiled back.

"OK?" he said.

"All right," she said.

He took hold of her jumper pinching it towards him. "Jeez, you're beautiful. I can smell that honeysuckle. Imagine us together in some little place. No kindergarten underfoot. No shocks. We could throw away the brandy bottle."

She took his hand rubbing his fingers. Her smile was so wide the strain left her eyes. But at that moment the phone rang.

"Jeez!" said Ted, "It's one of them!"

Joan went to silence the phone. It was in the living room and he heard her voice but caught no words. In a minute she was back pulling off her pullover. He saw her face when she threw it down.

"Who was it?" he said.

"Lois." She crossed her arms behind her back to unfasten her bra. Her hair was all over her shoulders.

"What did she want?"

"Nothing. She said she was coming."

"I knew she was coming. You said all of them were coming. What else was it?"

"Oh, Ted," she said sitting down and crossing her leg on her knee to take off her shoes. Her face had come loose too.

"Don't bother," Ted said, "I've lost interest. You have too. If you had any that is."

She sat still. Perhaps she hadn't heard him.

"I'll make us some tea and bring you a cup," she said.

"In advance of the brandy bottle. No thank you Joan."

She saw in the mirror his hooded eyes and set mouth.

"I think I'll go away alone," he said. "Up north alone."

"Don't be silly," she said.

"Don't talk to me as if I were Bramble, Joan."

This time she didn't correct him. She pulled on her pullover avoiding his eyes.

"I'll sell the taxi," Ted said, "You can have the house and I'll go north, I'll drive a cab for someone else."

She shut a drawer that wasn't really open. "You'll do no such thing Ted."

"I'll send you money but I won't send you love."

She put some lipstick on although she hadn't washed her face.

"I wouldn't want your money without your love."

He flung a leg towards her under the bedclothes. "For the last time Joan let's sell out and start a new life together away from them. We can tell them today we're going. See how they stand up to the shock."

"Oh Ted, she said smiling on him as if he were Bramwell.

"I mean it, Joan."

"You couldn't leave Wally now, could you?"

"I'm a traitor to Wally. I'm always lying to Wally. I told Wally I got four of the smartest, cleverest kids in Australia. Old Wally doesn't know the half of it."

"That's true what you say about the children," she said. He was silent looking more like a bulldog then. The kind she loved but was afraid to pat.

"You've never met Wally, have you? Wally and Bella."

"No, I haven't yet."

"Yet. Wally has been my best mate for years and you haven't got around to meeting him."

She sat down on the edge of the chair. "We'll have them for a meal sometime when we can organize it."

"You could come for a drink at the club and meet them there. Bella is more or less on tap since she's the barmaid. But you're too worn out after kindergarten and too frightened to leave the house in case one of them calls in for something or rings up for something."

"Oh Ted, you're hassling me."

"You're talking like them!"

Joan was silent a moment. "I'm worried," she said, "About Lois."

"I'm surprised. I thought you went along with all they did. They gave you no cause for worry."

She looked at the floor.

"I never got over Lois," Ted said. "This day I was saying to Wally 'I'll bring my girl Lois's school report in to show you what those teachers say about my smart kid.' That very evening you passed me the brandy bottle and a glass and told me to sit down. Because Lois had just gone off with Archie hitch-hiking around Australia. Seventeen and with one sleeping bag."

"I know. But all of them do it now. They go off to find themselves."

"Is that so? The only bright spot was that in the process of finding herself Lois lost Archie."

"And she came home to us, didn't she?"

"There was nowhere else to go."

Joan pressed her hands between her knees. Ted saw her face. "What about Lois? What did she say on the phone? What's she up to now?"

"Nothing."

"That's Lois. Nothing."

"Oh Ted, I don't mean she's doing nothing!"

"You just said she was doing nothing. She's done nothing since she left school."

"She's still working at those odd jobs. She lives with Cassandra." She looked at the floor. "But not much longer."

"Archie turned Lois off men for good. But why did she have to pick up with Cassandra?"

"Cassandra's met a man."

"A man wouldn't have met Cassandra. He would think it was another man."

"Cassandra is giving up the house. She and this man are buying a caravan and going around Australia. He makes jewellery from horseshoe nails. They're going to sell it in the country towns."

"What an affliction. The country people have got their own horseshoe nails. They don't want Cassandra's. And they've got their own problems. They don't deserve Cassandra."

"Ted! Stop talking about Cassandra. I want to tell you about Lois!"

"She rang to remind you to tell me, eh Joan? To prepare me before she comes? You've got to make sure the brandy bottle is on hand for me. Is that it Joan?" His voice had risen with his body out of the bed.

"Please, Ted!"

He dragged some clean underwear from a drawer. "Don't tell me! I don't want to know!"

"You've got to know! I've got to tell you!"

"No you don't! I'm going out for the day. I'm leaving you to them, Joan!"

243

She looked up at him but he was pulling on a singlet. "Don't be silly, Ted. What will they think if you're not here?"

"They mightn't notice. I'm going to find Wally. I'll have the day with Wally."

"Don't run out on me Ted!"

"You'll have them! You don't need me!"

"Oh Ted," she said wearily. "I do need you."

He was stumbling into underpants. "Like hell you need me! I know all about these family lunches." He dragged some shoes from the wardrobe and socks from a drawer. "There'll be steaks. I got plenty of memories of steaks for lunch. Two and a half pounds on Tim and Jerry's plates and half a pound on mine. Sometimes your conscience gets to you and you cover one of the pounds on their plates with a pound of mushrooms. I'm footing the bill for it all but there's enough room on my plate beside my steak to park my cab and Wally's."

"Stop it, Ted," she cried and he did because he saw her face so crumpled her hair looked too young for it. "It's Lois."

"Of course it's Lois! It's one of them all the time. It's all of them all the time. I've had as much as I can take. I'm going out to find Wally and we'll drink our way through a couple of dozen cans. That'll be my day."

"Ted!" Joan put both hands on the chair arms as if she needed help to stand. "Lois is into religion now."

"You talk like them!"

"All right. Lois is joining the Children of God."

"Jeez," said Ted standing still. "What are they?"

"It's a religious group. She's becoming one of them. A child of God."

"That finishes it. She doesn't want to be the child of Ted and Joan. She's denouncing us!"

"She's not! She's coming home to us!"

"What for this time?"

"To save some money."

Ted dropped shoes and socks on the floor. "Like hell she is! I'll take a stand. She's not coming here to stay. I'm not having Children of God in the lounge room and children of Ferdinand in the dining room! It's not on!" He seized a brush from the dressing table and began to brush his sparse grey hair. "It's just not on."

She put a hand out and touched his bare thigh and he jumped as if her fingers burned him. He stumped around the room finishing dressing. She stood up while he was jabbing a foot into a sock.

"I'm frightened of them too, you know Ted," she said.

He had one foot in the air and his eyes and mouth were three round rings focused on her. He lowered his leg. "Don't say that to me! Don't you dare say I'm frightened of them."

"I wouldn't say it if it wasn't true."

He jumped off the bed and went to the mirror and began to slap again at his hair with the brush. "Cut it out! They don't frighten me!" He pulled on a shirt and this ruffled his hair, so he seized the brush again.

"Oh, they do, Ted."

He threw the brush among the things on the dressing table. "They do not! I've never opened up on them because of you. You go along with all they do. You talk like them, you think like them!" He went to the wardrobe and pulled out a jacket and began to jerk into it. "I'm the outsider!"

He had his back to her and his bulldog neck seemed the loneliest thing she had ever seen. Her eyes filled with tears.

"I'll get right out," he said. "I'll leave you to them. You're just like them."

"Oh no Ted," she said. "Not me. You."

He gave her a swift unbelieving look. "Don't give me that! Bull like that!" But he looked in the mirror for reassurance. She met his eyes there.

"You're just like Tim. Just like Jerry. Restless like Lois. Looking for something Ted. I was too frightened once to look into your eyes." But in the mirror she was looking into them now.

"Eh?" he said reaching stupidly for the hair brush. "What?"

"Oh yes, Ted. Remember when you wanted to go away? I was too scared to go with you. I was too frightened to give up the house and your safe job. We could have tried it. I'm always thinking about it now."

"Don't," he said, slipping his eyes away from hers. "I never do."

"Oh, that's such a relief," she said sitting down and smiling so that tears ran down both cheeks.

"Don't cry," he said agonized, "I've made you cry!"

"You haven't," she said, wiping her eyes. "I like it."

He pulled her to her feet and she leaned against him. "Another thing," she said, "You give me so much strength."

"I do?" Ted looked in the mirror to check on himself. She had her cheek on his shoulder.

"Remember when Lois went off that time?"

"Jeez! Of course I do!"

"When you'd gone to work I used to sit and cry and cry."

"I didn't know!"

"One day Peggy—who used to live next door remember—dragged me off to this lunch to try and cheer me up. The speaker was a woman who had a lot to do with young people. She said when they do these strange things ask yourself, 'Is it wrong or is it different?'"

"I'd have told her!" Ted cried, "It's different—and it's wrong!"

"Of course," Joan said eyes closed cuddling into him.

"Eh?" said Ted, checking it out in the mirror.

"Oh Ted, I'm so frightened of what they might do next! But I can't oppose them, can I? When I don't understand it!"

"Well, I can!"

"I know. And when you rave and yell about it all I feel it's me getting it off my chest—"

"I shouldn't carry on," Ted said contritely rubbing a cheek on her forehead, "And make it all the harder for you. I'll try and remember not to."

"Oh keep it up," she said, "It makes it bearable. Do you understand?"

He wasn't listening that closely. He pulled her jumper off her shoulders and kissed her neck. "Jeez! Smell that honeysuckle! Do you have to do all those things for lunch?" he whispered.

"I can skip a few," she said, "Quite a few."

The doorbell rang and they sprang apart.

"Jeez!" Ted said. "We are scared of them!"

Joan wiped her eyes. "You see who it is. It's probably a doorknock collection."

She heard him cry out, "Jeez! Wal! Hallo, old son. This's a surprise. Come in!"

Ted appeared in the bedroom doorway with a man, smaller than he was, rather shrivelled looking with a too-red nose. He had a shabby overnight bag in one hand and cradled in the other arm were some cans of beer in a paper bag.

Ted was beaming with pride. Joan did not know if it was in her or Wally. "This is Joan, Wally," Ted said, "That's her!"

Joan gathered her loose hair with one hand and held the other out to Wally.

"Jeez!" Ted said, "You two have met at last!"

Wally's shy look followed his bag which he had dropped on the floor.

"Jeez!" Ted said, "What's up, old son? Is something wrong?"

Wally was silent and Joan pushed a chair forward for him to sit.

Ted and Joan waited for him to speak. "The worst happened, Ted. Bella kicked me out!"

"Bella did!" Ted was astounded.

"Not really Bella, Bella's rotten bludger of a son. He turned up last night out of the blue and said I had to go."

"He can't do that!" Ted said.

"Bella didn't stop him," Wally said with a shaking mouth looking at the window then down at his bag. "I grabbed a few things and went. I got me cans out of the fridge. I wasn't leaving them for him. He said I'd sponged on his mother long enough."

"He can't do that," Ted said "You're married to Bella."

"We been together ten years," Wally said, "Not married. I should've said. I didn't."

"Forget it, old son," Ted said, "What's a slip of paper?"

"That's what Bella and I used to say."

"Jeez Wal, I'm sorry old son," Ted said, "I'd like to say stay here. But our girl Lois is coming home for a bit. Isn't she Joan?"

"Wally can stay for lunch," Joan said.

"Jeez, so he can!" said Ted. "The kids are coming. You can meet them, Wal!"

"Oh jeez, Ted," Wally said wiping his eyes with the back of his hand. "Half your luck! A great missus and all those beaut kids! I don't think I could stay, Ted!"

"Of course you can!" Ted said, "You can have my steak. A few scraggy ends'll do me!" He took the beer from Wally's lap and handed it to Joan. "Put those in the fridge for Wal, Joan. And bring the brandy bottle and a glass. Poor old Wal. He's had a shock!"

My Father sat at the kitchen table much longer than he should have talking about Clarice Carmody coming to Berrigo.

My mother got restless because of the cigarettes my father was rolling and smoking. She worked extra fast glancing several times pointedly through the doorway at the waving corn paddock which my father had come from earlier than he need have for morning tea.

He creaked the kitchen chair as he talked especially when he said her name.

"Clarice Carmody! Sounds like one of them Tivoli dancers!"

My mother put another piece of wood in the stove.

"God help Jack Patterson, that's all I can say," my father said. My mother's face wore an expression that said she wished it was.

"A mail order marriage!" my father said putting his tobacco tin in his hip pocket. Suddenly he laughed so loud my mother turned around at the dresser.

"That's a good one!" he said, slapping his tongue on his cigarette paper with is brown eyes shining.

My mother strutted to the stove on her short fat legs to put the big kettle over the heat.

"It might be too," she said.

"Might be what too?" my father said, almost but not quite mocking her.

"A good marriage," my mother said, emptying the teapot into the scrap bucket which seemed another way of saying morning tea time was over.

"They've never set eyes on each other!" my father said. "They wouldn't know each other's faults . . ."

"They'll soon learn them," my mother said dumping the biscuit tin on the dresser top after clamping the lid on.

The next sound was a clamping noise too. My father crossed the floor on the way out almost treading on me sitting on the doorstep.

"Out of the damn way!" he said, quite angry.

My mother sat on a chair for a few moments after he'd gone watching through the doorway with the hint of a smile which vanished when her eyes fell on me.

"You could be out there giving him a hand," she said.

My toe began to smart a little where his big boots grazed it.

I bit at my kneecaps hoping my mother would say no more on the idea.

She didn't. She began to scrape new potatoes splashing them in a bowl of water.

Perhaps she was thinking about Clarice Carmody. I was. I was seeing her dancing on the stage of the old School of Arts. I thought of thistledown lifted off the ground and bowling along when you don't believe there is a wind. In my excitement I wrapped my arms around my knees and licked them.

"Stop that dirty habit," my mother said. "Surely there is something you could be doing."

"Will we visit Clarice Carmody?" I asked.

"She won't be Clarice Carmody," my mother said, vigorously rinsing a potato. "She'll be Clarice Patterson."

She sounded different already.

She came to Berrigo at the start of the September school holidays.

"The spring and I came together!" she said to me when at last I got to see her at home.

She and Jack Patterson moved into the empty place on the Patterson's farm where a farm hand and his family lived when the Patterson children were little. When the

253

two boys left school they milked and ploughed and cleared the bush with old Bert Patterson the father. The girl Mary went to the city to work in an office which sounded a wonderful life to me. Cecil Patterson the younger son married Elsie Clark and brought her to the big old Patterson house to live. Young Mrs Patterson had plenty to do as old Mrs Patterson took to her bed when another woman came into the house saying her legs went.

My father was always planning means of tricking old Mrs Patterson into using her legs, like letting a fire get out of control on Berrigo sports day, or raising the alarm on Berrigo picture night.

For old Mrs Patterson's disability didn't prevent her from going to everything that was on in Berrigo carried from the Patterson's car by Jack and Cecil. Immediately she was set down, to make up for the time spent in isolation on the farm where Elsie took out her resentment with long sulky silences, she turned her fat, creamy face to left and right looking for people to talk to.

Right off she would say "not a peep out of the silly things" when asked about her legs.

My father who called her a parasite and a sponger would sit in the kitchen after meals and roll and smoke his cigarettes while he worked out plans for making her get up and run.

My mother sweeping his saucer away while his cup was in midair said more than once good luck to

Gladdie Patterson, she was the smartest woman in Berrigo, and my father silenced would get up after a while and go back to work.

Jack Patterson went to the city and brought Clarice back. My father said how was anyone to know whether they were married or not and my mother said where was the great disadvantage in not being married? My father's glance fell on the old grey shirt of his she was mending and he got up very soon and clumped off to the corn paddock.

I tried to see now by looking at Clarice whether she was married to Jack Patterson. She wore a gold ring which looked a bit loose on her finger. My father having lost no time in getting a look at Clarice when she first arrived said it was one of Mrs Patterson's old rings or perhaps he said one of old Mrs Patterson's rings. He described Clarice as resembling "one of them long armed golliwog doils kids play with." Then he added with one of his short quick laughs that she would be about as much use to Jack Patterson as a doll.

The wedding ring Clarice wore didn't seem to match her narrow hand. I saw it plainly when she dug her finger into the jar of jam I'd brought her.

Her mouth and eyes went round like three Os. She waggled her head and her heavy frizzy hair shook.

"Lovely, darlink," she said. "You must have the cleverest, kindest mother in the whole of the world."

255

I blushed at this inaccurate description of my mother and hoped the two would not meet up too soon for Clarice to be disappointed.

Sitting there on one of her kitchen chairs, which like all the other furniture were leftovers from the big house, I did not want ever to see Clarice disappointed.

My hopes were short-lived. Jack Patterson came in then and Clarice's face and all her body changed. She did look a little like a golliwog doll although her long arms were mostly gracefully loose. Now she seemed awkward putting her hand on the kettle handle, looking towards Jack as if asking should she be making tea. Both Jack and I looked at the table with several dirty cups and saucers on it. Jack looked over my head out the window. Clarice walked in a stiff-legged way to the table and picked up the jam.

"Look!" she said holding it to the light. "The lovely colour! Jam red!" Jack Patterson had seen plenty of jam so you couldn't expect him to be impressed. He half hung his head and Clarice tried again.

"This is Ellen from across the creek! Oh, goodness me! I shouldn't go round introducing people! Everyone knows everyone in the country!"

Jack Patterson took his yard hat and went out.

"Oh, darlink!" Clarice said in a defeated way putting the jam on the shelf above the stove. I wanted to tell her that wasn't where you kept the jam but didn't dare.

She sat on a chair with her feet forward, the skirt of her dress reaching to her calves. She looked straight at me, smiling and crinkling her eyes.

"I think, darlink," she said, "you and I are going to be really great friends."

People said that in books. Here was Clarice saying it to me. She had mentioned introducing me too, which was something happening to me for the first time in my life. I was happy enough for my heart to burst through my skinny ribs.

But I had to get off the chair and go home. My mother said I was to give her the jam and go.

But she asked me about Clarice and Jack Patterson as if she expected me to observe things while I was there. "What's the place like?" she said.

I remembered the dark little hall and the open bedroom door showing the bed not made and clothes hanging from the brass knobs and the floor mat wrinkled. And Clarice with her halo of frizzy hair and her wide smile drawing me down the hall to her.

"She's got it fixed up pretty good," I lied.

"The work all done?" my mother asked.

I said yes because I felt Clarice had done all the work she intended to do for that day anyway.

I felt unhappy for Clarice because the Berrigo women most looked up to were those who got their housework done early and kept their homes neat all the time.

I next saw Clarice two months later at Berrigo show.

She wore a dress of soft green material with a band of the same stuff holding her wild hair above her forehead.

"Look!" said Merle Adcock, who was eighteen and dressed from Winn's mail order catalogue. "She got her belt tied round her head!"

Clarice had her arm through Jack Patterson's, which also drew scornful looks from Berrigo people. When Jack Patterson talked to other men about the prize cows and bulls Clarice stayed there, and watching them I was pretty sure Jack would have liked to have shaken Clarice's arm off.

My mother worked all day in the food tent at the show but managed to get what Berrigo called "a good gander" at Clarice with Jack.

"A wife hasn't made a difference to Jack Patterson," she said at home that afternoon. "He looks as hang dog as ever."

My father, to my surprise and perhaps to hers too, got up at once and went off to the yard.

The sports day was the week after the show and that was when my father and Clarice met.

Clarice saw me and said "Hello, darlink" and laid a finger on my nose to flatten the turned up end. She laughed when she did it so my feelings wouldn't be hurt.

My father suddenly appeared behind us.

I was about to scuttle off thinking that was why he was there, but he stood in a kind of strutting pose looking at Clarice and putting a hand on the crown of my hat.

"I'm this little one's Dad," he said, "She could introduce us."

I was struck silent by his touch and by his voice with a teasing note in it, so I couldn't have introduced them even if practised at it.

"Everyone is staring at me," Clarice said. "So they know who I am."

"Berrigo always stares," said my father taking out his tobacco tin and cigarette papers and staring at Clarice too.

She lifted her chin and looked at him with all her face in a way she had. "Like the cows," she said and laughed.

Her glance fell on his hands rolling his smoke, so different from my mother's expression. I thought smoking was sinful but started to change my ideas seeing Clarice's lively interested eyes and smiling mouth.

"Your father was talking to Clarice Carmody," my mother said at home after the sports as if it was my fault.

I noticed she said Clarice Carmody, not Clarice Patterson and perhaps she read my thoughts.

"I doubt very much that she's Clarice Patterson," my mother said, hanging up the potholder with a jab.

I felt troubled. First it was my father who seemed opposed to Clarice. Now it was my mother. I wondered how I would get to see her.

My chance came when I least expected it. My mother sent me with the slide normally used to take the cans of cream to the roadside to be picked up by the cream lorry, to load with dry sticks to get the stove and copper fire going.

The shivery grass was blowing and I was imagining it was the sea which I had never seen, and the slide was a ship sailing through it.

Clarice was standing there in the bush as if she had dropped from the sky.

"Darlink!" she called stalking towards me holding her dress away from the tussocks and blackberries sprouting up beside the track which led down to the creek separating Patterson's from our place.

"It's so hot, darlink isn't it?" she said lifting her mop of hair for the air to get through it.

No one else looked at me the way Clarice did with her smiling mouth, wrinkling nose and crinkling eyes. I hoped she didn't find me too awful with straight hair and skin off my sunburned nose and a dress not even fit to wear to school.

She put out a finger and pressed my nose and laughed.

"Why don't we go for a swim, darlink?" she said.

Behind her below the bank of blackberries there was a waterhole. A tree felled years and years ago and bleached white as a bone made a bridge across the creek. The water banked up behind it so it was deep on one side and just a trickle on the other.

I wasn't allowed to swim there. In fact I couldn't swim and neither could any other girls in Berrigo my age. The teacher at school who was a man took the boys swimming in the hole but there was no woman to take the girls so we sat on the school verandah and read what we liked from the school bookshelf supervised by Cissy Adcock the oldest girl in the school.

But how could I tell Clarice I couldn't swim much less take my clothes off? I would certainly be in for what my mother called the father of a belting for such a crime.

"I'll swim and you can cool your tootsies," Clarice said throwing an arm around me.

We walked down the track crushed together, me thinking already of looking back on this wonderful change of events, but worried about my bony frame not responding to her embrace.

She let go of me near the bank and stepping forward a pace or two began to take off her clothes.

One piece after another.

She lifted her dress and petticoat over her head and cast them onto the branch of a sapling gum. Her hands came around behind her unhooking her brassiere which was something I dreamed of wearing one day and threw it after her other things. When she bent and raised one leg to take off her pants I thought she looked

261

like a young tree. Not a tree everyone would say was beautiful but a tree you would look at more than once.

She jumped into the water ducking down till it covered her to the neck which she swung around to look at me.

"Oh, you should come in, darlink!" she said. She lifted both her arms and the water as if reluctant to let go of her flowed off them.

"Watch, darlink," she said and swam, flicking her face from side to side, churning up the water with her white legs. She laughed when she reached the other bank so quickly because the hole was so small.

She sat on a half submerged log and lifting handfuls of mud rubbed it into her thighs.

"Very healthy, darlink," she said without looking at my shocked face.

She rubbed it on her arms and shoulders and it ran in little grey dollops between her breasts.

Then she plunged in and swam across to me. She came up beside me slipping a bit and laughing.

"That was wonderful, darlink," she said a little wistfully though, as if she doubted she would ever do it again.

The bush was quiet, so silent you could hear your own breath until a bird called and Clarice jumped a little.

"That's a whip bird," I said hearing it again a little further away, the sound of a whip lashed in the air.

"Oh darlink, you are so clever," she said and began to get dressed.

No one at home noticed I'd been away too long. My father was dawdling over afternoon tea just before milking and my mother bustling about made a clicking noise with her tongue every time a cow bellowed.

"It's no life for a girl," my father said referring to Clarice and making me jump nervously as if there was a way of detecting what we'd been up to.

"She took it on herself," said my mother, prodding at some corned beef in a saucepan on the stove.

"I'll bet they never let on to her about old lolly legs," said my father slapping away almost savagely with his tongue on his cigarette paper. "Landing a young girl into that! They'll expect her to wait on that old sponger before too long."

He put his tobacco away. "I'll bet Jack Patterson hardly says a word to her from one week's end to the next." He stared at his smoke. "Let alone anything else."

My mother straightened up from the stove. Her sweaty hair was spikey around her red face which wore a pinched and anxious expression, perhaps because of the late start on the milking. She crushed her old yard hat on.

"I'll go and start," she said.

My father smoked on for a minute or two then got up and looked around the kitchen as if seeing it for the first time.

He reached for his yard hat and put it on.

"What do you think of Clarice?" he said.

I laid my face on my knees to hide my guilt.

"She's beautiful," I said.

When he stomped past me sitting on the step he kept quite clear to avoid stepping on me.

I got a chance to go and see Clarice one day in the Christmas holidays when my mother went into Berrigo to buy fruit for the Christmas cake and cordial essence.

Clarice put her arm around me standing at the window watching Elsie Patterson at the clothesline.

Elsie was football shaped under her apron and she carefully unpegged shirts and dresses, turning them around and pegging them again. She took the sides of towels and tea towels between her hands and stretched them even.

"Why does she do that, darlink?" Clarice asked me.

Berrigo women were proud of their wash, but I found this hard to explain to Clarice.

She laughed merrily when we turned away. "People are so funny, aren't they darlink?"

She suggested going for a swim because the day was what my mother called a roaster.

This time she took off all her underwear at home leaving her thin dress showing her shape.

"Oh, darlink!" she said when I looked away.

I followed her round bottom with a couple of lovely little dents in it down to the waterhole.

The bush was not as quiet as before. Someone is about, I thought with a bush child's instinct for such things.

"I'll go and watch in case someone comes," I said, and she threw a handful of water at me for my foolishness.

I ran a little way up the track and when I lifted my head there shielded by some saplings astride his horse was my father.

I stopped so close the flesh of the horse's chest quivered near my eyes.

"Don't go any further," I said. "Clarice is swimming."

My father jumped off the horse and tied the bridle to a tree.

"Go on home," he said. But I didn't move.

"Go on!" he said and I moved off too slowly. He picked up a piece of chunky wood and threw it.

The horse plunged and the wood glanced off my arm as I ran.

At home I beat at the fire in the stove with the poker and put the kettle over the heat relieved when it started to sing.

I went to the kitchen door and my mother was coming down the track from the road. I heard Tingle's bus which went in and out of Berrigo every day go whining along the main road after dropping her off.

265

She had both arms held away from her body with parcels hanging from them.

I went to meet her not looking at her face but seeing it all the same red under the grey coloured straw hat with the bunch of violets on the brim. She had had the hat a long time.

String from the parcels was wound around her fingers and it was hard to free them.

"Be careful!" she said, hot and angry. "Don't drop that one!"

When she was inside and saw the fire going and the kettle near the boil she spoke more gently.

"It's a shaving mug," she said, hiding the little parcel in the back of the dresser. "For your father for Christmas."

The child came into the room bending her body towards the old woman in bed. The room was actually the child's and the old woman's, but the latter's illness made it necessary for the child to sleep on the lounge.

The lounge was the old-fashioned kind eventually to be discarded and the sloping back caused the child to wake up when she turned over and hit her face against it.

She dreamed once she was being crushed by a hill caving in but she did not tell her mother because she knew what the reaction would be.

"Hear that, Barry!" the mother would have said to her husband, the old woman's son. "She can't get a proper night's rest. She needs her own bed!"

Her husband would twitch his body, indicating he had heard (and agreed) and would pull his face in, losing

267

more of his chin, of which he had very little. He was a slight man with skin and hair of a washed-out colour, like separated milk.

"Barry looks like the milk at that factory where he works," the old woman often said to herself. "Drained of all its strength."

So the child very quietly would fold her blanket and sheet each morning and put them under the loose cushions on the lounge and put her nightdress in a drawer in her room.

She had the nightdress now to put away before she left for school.

"Can I bring you anything, Granma?" she said.

The old woman moved her head on the pillow. The bedclothes were tight across her except for a little hollow where her mouth was. The child moved closer and peered into the hollow to judge better how ill the old woman was.

"Granma?" said the child.

"Nothing," the old woman said. "I'll be better soon and you can come back to your own little bed again. I only put the light on twice last night."

"Only twice!" the child marvelled as if she were the adult and the old woman the child.

"Once to take a pill, and once for a drink of water. I knocked the glass over, but it dried up I think. Take a little look and see if it dried up, will you?" The old woman's whispering voice lost its strength, like wind passing through dried grass.

The child felt the table and moved a package containing the old woman's pension card, and covered some dampness with it.

"Are you going to school now?" the old woman said. The child was in her check dress with her hair newly done and the ribbons pulling it upwards from her ears so it was obvious she was.

But the two talked to each other this way.

"You've got your brown cardigan on, Granma," the child would say. The old woman's frame had shrunk since she bought the cardigan ten years before, and wearing it now she had the appearance of a peg doll dressed in something too big for it.

"Ah, stupid!" the child's brother would say, lunging out a leg and kicking her, and the mother's face would tighten and her eyes flash agreeing that she was.

Embarrassed the child would raise her rump higher and lower her head over her book on the floor and colour in with more vigour. The old woman's hand crunched on her knee would want to reach out and touch the child's hair.

Now the old woman wanted to take hold of the child's hand hanging loose with the nightdress under one arm.

But her own arms were bound to her sides in bed.

The way she makes a bed, the old woman thought shutting her eyes against a picture of her daughter-in-law stretching the tugging and tightening the covers, so the old woman had to wriggle her way into bed leaving her nightdress well above her waist.

"Granma?" the child said again.

"Nothing," whispered the old woman and struggled in her mind to find something to share with the child. Without looking she knew the bright blue of the child's eyes would be distinct from the white.

"Put your nightie away," the old woman said glad to have thought of that.

The child was crunching it into a drawer when the mother came into the room.

"Don't do it that way!" she cried. "Don't squash and wrinkle up everything!" She snatched up the nightie, rearranged the other clothing, and folding the nightie flat laid it down one end. She slammed the drawer shut going tch-tch with her tongue as if to say here was something more disrupting the place.

She lingered at the dressing table, changing expression at the sight of herself in the mirror. Few would guess to look at her that she worked on a delicatessen counter, discarding her outdoor clothing when she arrived at work for a white overall and cap. She wore a long black skirt that swished about the top of her black boots, an imitation fur jacket and cap to match. Her hair had a red rinse which she was sure no one detected, and it was cut in such a way two ends lay in spikes on her cheeks, matching her spikey fringe.

She turned her head admiring her profile but frowned when her eyes met the eyes of the old woman reflected in the glass.

She can't escape me, the old woman thought turning away.

"Get your schoolcase and things," the mother said to the child, not looking at her but pinching and plucking her coat about the shoulders and stroking and twisting the hair spikes.

"Well, go *on*," she said with irritation, and the child scuttled ahead of her out of the room.

"I'll shut this," the mother said loudly as if the old woman was deaf.

The child's eyes, like a piece of blue sky, showed briefly in the crack before the door closed with a snap.

The old woman heard the mother's boots and the child's school shoes tap down the steps and quicken on the footpath then lost in the noise of the traffic.

Peace fell on the old woman's face like pale sun but there was no sun. She ran her tongue inside her dry mouth.

"I'll get up and move around and get my sweat going," she said feeling an itch of her dry skin.

The wardrobe door was closed on her dressing gown. Her daughter-in-law could not bear the sight of anything scattered on the floors so her slippers were out of sight too.

"Bugger me. I haven't got the strength to get them," she said.

"But I'm not laying here. You rot in bed."

She got her feet out and swung them above a small bedside mat.

"Japanese rubbish," she said looking down at it.

She stood up gingerly.

"Weak as a cat," she whispered, staring at the door, willing it to come closer.

Pins and needles raced up her legs. But she trotted forward and opened the door onto the carpet in the hall. The carpet was an off-white colour put down from earnings at the delicatessen. The daughter-in-law treated it with reverence. Coming home each day her eyes fell on it for marks. Leaving each morning she sometimes took a brush and kneeling in her good clothes brushed the pile upright. Now the old woman wished she could avoid walking on it. She felt so heavy she was sure every footstep would flatten it. But she was so light she wafted across it like thistledown in her billowing flannelette nightgown.

In the living room she took hold of two chair arms, turned herself around and sat down.

"Ah," she said, pleased at the achievement and putting her head back. It rested on one of the daughter-in-law's cushions and immediately she snapped her head forward. She had heard the daughter-in-law's boots pummelling the floor that morning as she went through the ritual of straightening mats, fixing cushions and pulling chairs to the angle she wanted them.

The old woman crossed her legs and began to rock a foot. The foot was a purplish brown colour like her leg covered with hundreds of little criss cross lines. She thought of the child's legs as she saw them that morning above her white school socks. Like fawn satin, she thought holding the memory under her shut eyes. She slept a little because she opened her eyes surprised at the sight of the living room furniture.

All those sharp edges, she thought, feeling as if they were cutting her. The daughter-in-law always rubbed fiercely at the edges of tables and chairs with her polishing cloth as if she wanted to turn them into weapons. The old woman remembered the furniture at the old place. There was the fat old sideboard crowded with sepia pictures, the cruet set, water jug and glasses.

"Damn rubbish," Barry had said for his wife who looked sharp and ferret-like on that last day.

There was a little tapping noise and the old woman opened her eyes. The venetian blind had swung around in a small wind from the window and speared at the air with its slats.

"Those things," the old woman said with scorn.

"Give me my old red curtains any day."

She saw them burning in the back yard and Barry walking around throwing sticks and leaves on the fire to make them go faster. One of the tassels had blown away and burned out lying a little away from the fire.

She remembered it shaped like a little bell in ashes on the green grass.

"Pretty," she said, wondering why she hadn't shown it to the child.

Why hadn't she? Where was the child that day? Had she been born then? Agitated she rocked her foot harder, plucking through loose ends in her brain to get events in order.

"You went to Hilda straight after the old place was sold," she said stern with her muddled brain.

She saw them together, two old bandy legged women struggling up a hill in the wind to buy cat food and indigestion powder (Hilda really had cancer and died and it was decided then that the old woman's two sons should have her turn about for six months).

She saw herself waiting with Barry for a train to take her to Corrimal where she was to spend the first six months with Percy, the other son.

"You'll like it there," Barry said when a great hiss and puff from the engine had died away.

"You can go and sit on the beach whenever you want to."

The old woman remembered the wind lifting the sand and flinging it against her face. She saw Percy's wife making ridges in it with her hands. The two boys blue like skinned rabbits in wet trunks were hunched over sniffing in the cold. All of them were set apart reminding the old woman of gnomes in a garden.

They all looked out to sea as if to find the answers there.

Five months and four days after going to Percy she came to Barry because Percy had been given his holidays (he said) and her time was nearly up anyway.

She saw herself waiting with Percy for the train to Sydney. His wife was already getting the room ready for the younger of the boys.

"You're only a spit from all the shops," Percy said. "You'll like it there."

She looked down remembering how she stood with only one case. When she went to Hilda she had three. What happened to the other two?

"Bugger me. They must have got lost somewhere," the old woman said.

She rocked her foot and dozed. She must have dozed because she opened her eyes and Barry was there rolling a cigarette between his blue white fingers. In his job he started at dawn and came home at midday.

Licking the cigarette paper Barry saw a picture crooked and went and straightened it.

"Damn kids," he said. "Jumpin' about the way they do. Wreck a place."

He sat on a chair well forward to smoke.

The old woman with her head forward to avoid touching the cushion was so still she might have been a drawing.

"You still crook?" Barry said.

"Not too bad," the old woman said.

She rocked her foot and Barry smoked. Then he screwed his rump around to put his tobacco in a back pocket.

"You ought to go into one of them places," he said.

The old woman halted her rocking foot. She took hold, of the two chair arms. She had a vision of a row of beds with grey haired women in them. The floor was a vast slippery sea. She was struggling from one of the beds, made tight like the daughter-in-law's beds, to look for a lavatory.

"I'd need more strength," the old woman said.

"They take you sick," Barry said. "Sick or well they take you. We've seen one. Clean. God, it's clean."

Now? wondered the old woman and didn't know whether she spoke or not.

She thought of the child running home. Her shoes on the steps, tap, tap, tap. Her schoolcase banging the rails in her haste. She thought of all the child, her blocky little shape and those legs and arms and that fair, springy hair.

But not the eyes, bright blue inside all that white.

She dropped her head back on the daughter-in-law's cushion.

"Well, bugger me if I care," the old woman said.

THE SEA ON A SUNDAY

All the summer the cars tore to the sea between milkings on a Sunday.

The Went children watched from the verandah of their house built close to the road.

It was rented to them by the Manns, quite well off property owners who built it originally for one of the families they employed. But they later built homes near the main homestead for sons who married. The sons did the work previously done by employed labour so the road house as they called it became obsolete.

It had a verandah along the front and four rooms, two front and two back. One was a kitchen and all the others bedrooms although one of the front rooms, the one you stepped into from the verandah doubled as a sitting room. Anyone calling during the day sat on one of the two stretchers against the wall and if it was night they were taken through to the kitchen where a stove burned all the year round.

There were also two stretchers on the verandah one either side of the front door which Mrs Went kept neatly made the moment they were vacated by little Wents. The pillows were plumped up and the quilts smoothed out without a crease. Sometimes the wind whipped the covers about showing the shabby stretcher legs and Mrs Went would hurry out and smooth them out again, treating the bed like brazen daughters with their skirts raised.

The reason for all the beds at the Wents was the seven children aged between twelve and two.

They had no car and it was very often hard to find the rent for Arthur Mann when he rode up for it at the end of each month and there was no way in the world the Wents could get to the sea on a Sunday.

Their house was three miles outside the town and the sea another twelve miles off.

Since most people were small farmers it was their cars the Wents watched tearing through the dust and rocking on the gravel as they rushed to the sea.

It was one of the complexities of life that in summer the cows gave more generously of their milk and in summer with the sun at its hottest the sweaty bodies of the farming families longed for the relief of the sea.

They mostly rose as soon as it was light and raced through the dairy work with a speed similar to that of their cars racing to the sea.

They went without a meal after the milking (second breakfast it was called) and if their strength permitted raced into the water as soon as they arrived (although the weather had a devilish habit of turning bleak as soon as the old Fords and Austins and Dodges pulled up on the grassy slope just above the beach). The wives and elder girls were left to get the food spread out and ready after the first swim.

The Wents had no cows to milk and plenty of time for the sea on a Sunday but no money for swimming costumes and no means of transport and one of the children looking around the room one day wondered privately what they would pack their food in if through some miracle they got there.

It seemed pretty certain that the best for them was to line up on the verandah, feet dangling into the geraniums and watch the cars go past.

The verandah beds would be made long before the first car rumbled in the distance and the verandah swept and the folded cornbag shaken and laid neatly at the front door which was open to show the front room tidy, sometimes with a jug of gum tips on the mantlepiece. Mrs Went let a corner of a small table be seen tantalizing the passersby into wondering what other furniture had crowded it out, while the fact was apart from the beds it was the only furniture in the room. You could not count the stack of old suitcases in one corner that held some Went clothing (the top ones) and clothes not presently in circulation (the large bottom one).

Mrs Went swept the path too and scolded the young Wents soundly if they left the old wooden gate swinging on its hinges instead of closed with the hoop of wire holding it to the post.

Around half past ten with the fowls chased from the sagging wire fence that ran down the side of the house because they tended to squeeze in and foul both the path and the roots of the lemon tree the Wents were ranged along the verandah edge waiting for the first car.

Mrs Went took herself to the kitchen to start getting midday dinner ready. Mr Went would be there sitting on the old couch not too far from the fire, a strange habit for the summertime and stranger still was his attire of a flannel the colour of dirty milk and thick socks with working boots.

In spite of the boots Mr Went did not often work. He was a very talkative man and when Mrs Went trotted out to see a car go by urged on by yells from the children he (with much effort) would slide along the couch to poke his head around the door and stare his disapproval at the interruption.

She would return apologetic to resume her potato peeling as soon as the road was quiet again.

280

"They wanted me to see the Bartons," she would say. (Or the Boxalls, the Gillespies, the Skinners, the Percy Henrys or one of the Turner families.)

This being a typical Sunday morning (so far) Horrie Went then launched into a harangue about the family in the car on its way to the sea.

No matter who it was they had no right to be going there.

"The Bartons!" he cried standing up for better effect and putting a long piece of twisted paper in the stove to light his cigarette. For despite the terrible struggle for the Wents to exist from week to week Horrie still indulged his desire to smoke almost continuously. Mrs Went (Bertha) may privately disagree with him about the Bartons and some of the others but she would listen and use some soothing words when Horrie became overheated.

"Clyde Barton!" cried Horrie not sitting down immediately which showed how strongly he felt, "He got that farm because his father was a cattle thief!"

"A cattle thief!" he repeated and Bertha having heard the story every time the Bartons went past to the sea on a Sunday had to pretend she was hearing it all for the first time to build up enthusiastic responses.

She thought the fact that Clyde Barton's father long dead made some profit cattle duffing was not all that relevant to the present conditions for the Bartons who struggled as hard as any of the small farmers and restricted their time at the sea on a Sunday to less than three hours fearing any reckless treatment of the cows like milking them too late or too early and hastening the operation would affect their productivity.

Here was another point that called for scorn from Horrie.

In one way or another the Bartons, the Turners, the Skinners and others were putting pleasure before duty by indulging their fondness for the sea on a Sunday.

Particularly the Turners devout Catholics before the advent of the motor car and now almost every Sunday their old Rugby sailed past swarming with esctatic children waving from the spaces where side curtains should have been.

The Turners bypassed Mass all the year round being too ashamed to draw attention to a display of seasonal devotion by attending in the winter and all of this irked Horrie to boiling point although he himself was a Catholic. Winter or summer he did not step inside a church the excuse being lack of Sunday clothes and no car.

"Look at them! I don't want to look at them!" cried Horrie when the young Wents shouted that the Turners were coming and Mrs Went went trotting.

When she returned Horrie had worked himself into an emotional state.

"That Godless lot!" he cried making a fresh cigarette when the other was not completely smoked.

He flung down his dead match and Bertha flinched as Horrie could have used a light from the stove and saved on the box.

"It's a wonder they're not struck down in the water! How could they be enjoyin' themselves? They couldn't enjoy themselves with that on their conscience!"

Bertha thought of the blue sea gently lapping the white sands of Short Point which was the name of the beach and the little Turners running and squealing on the edge.

Horrie sank down into the corner of the couch with his eyes on the fire and his cigarette burning between his fingers on a raised knee in old grey serge pants.

She wanted to say "Never mind, love," but did not quite know what he should not be minding.

Then there was a shriek from the verandah that another car was coming but Bertha called out that she had her hands in flour.

"Them kids shouldn't be out there on that verandah Sunday after Sunday!" said Horrie.

Bertha preferred them there to under her feet and rather enjoying the variety that Sunday brought tried without success to think of something to distract Horrie and get him back to his moody smoking.

Her heart sank when he got up and used a match again to re-light his cigarette.

"A man should put a stop to it!" he said.

"It's like cheerin' them on at a football match!"

He was not going to sit down again it appeared.

"It's just like they're winnin' something! Winning!" cried Horrie.

He went through the house to lean in the front doorway and contemplate the backs of the young Wents on the verandah. Seven faces turned to look at him. All of them were happy.

"Hullo, Dad," most of them said although they had sat with him at breakfast.

No car was coming then and the Wents were threshing their feet about among the geraniums rather like cooling and splashing them in the sea.

"Youse are breaking them plants doin' that!" Horrie said and the young Wents stilled their feet.

Mrs Went heard Horrie's raised voice and called from the kitchen. "Are any of them sittin' on the beds?" No greater Sunday morning crime was known to Bertha than sitting on the verandah beds.

She trotted out evidently done with the flour to join Horrie in the doorway and look to the left for the sight or sound of a car on its way to the sea.

The eldest Went child a girl named Katie brought Bertha up to date.

"The Skinners just went," she said.

"Was Granny Skinner there?" asked Bertha.

"Granny Skinner!" cried Horrie walking to the end of the verandah where Bertha had trained a grape vine to cut off the heat from the western sun.

The eyes of the seven young Wents were on the back of his neck.

"What I could tell you about Granny Skinner!" said Horrie and the young Wents waited.

Horrie stared into the grape vine assembling his words for the best effect.

Then he turned around as if ready and rocking himself on his working boots stared into the verandah ceiling where rust was spreading along a join in the iron.

But there was a spurt of noise in the distance and every young Went head swung to the left and every pair of feet with Horrie's warning forgotten beat the geraniums and every pair of ears were strained and the squealing held back to come out of seven throats in a thin excited pipe.

"One's coming!" cried Errol the second youngest glad to be the first to say it.

"Who do you say it is?" cried Jimmy the second eldest. "Everyone have a guess!"

They called out the Grants, the Gillespies, the Boxalls (forgetting the Boxalls had already gone) and the Henrys and then there was an argument because Jimmy said the Henrys and Katie said he meant the Percy Henrys but it turned out to be the Hector Henrys.

"I just said Henrys and its Henrys!" cried Jimmy.

"You meant the Percy Henrys because the Hector Henrys never go to the sea on a Sunday!" said Katie.

Bertha hushed them because the car was bumping through the belt of gums and she wanted to concentrate on the unusual spectecle of the Hector Henrys on the way to the sea in their old navy blue Buick.

The car had obviously been successfully tinkered with by the oldest Henry boys Mickey and Joe who had been working on it since the summer started and here it was returning thanks for their labours by actually going, not at any breakneck speed but toiling along with Joe at the wheel holding it so hard his face paled as if this was a way of pumping life into the laconic engine.

The car was level with the corner of the Went's front yard when it slowed down and hopped like a wounded animal trying valiantly to make the distance. With each hop Mrs Henry and the three daughters in the back seat swooped from the waist up as if they had performed on the stage and the show was now over. Joe was clinging so hard to the wheel it appeared that it would take more than human effort to extract him.

The Wents on the verandah were utterly silenced.

Always the cars had appeared to speed up passing the house with the unspoken cry of look-where-we're-going-and-you're-not and the excited shrieks of the Wents pleading to slow down had been lost in the roar of the engine.

Here was silence and a car actually stopped.

They all looked to Horrie for instructions on what to do and Bertha stepped back and stopped herself in time from sitting on one of the verandah beds and looked at Horrie too and waited.

Not for long:

Horrie as if injected with the life that left the engine of the Henry's car ran down the verandah steps and let himself out of the gate leaving it swinging in his haste to reach Hector's side with a hand extended.

He shook Hector's hand vigorously and laid his free hand on Hector's shoulder.

Hector had his chin dropped onto his collar and Mrs Henry and the girls were in a little group as if assembled to be photographed although wearing expressions of doom.

Mickey and Joe were staring into the engine of the Buick.

"I knew it! I knew!" said Hector.

"The old bastard!" muttered Mickey to Joe. "He wouldn't know a big end from the axle!"

"Hit him over the head with the jack," Joe muttered back.

They had their dark rather handsome heads together under the bonnet.

"We'll find a place to sit in the shade," called Mrs Henry moving towards the bank opposite the Went's house.

"Indeed you won't!" said Horrie looking to the verandah and Bertha.

"Come up onto the verandah! Make room there you kids!"

The puzzled young Wents rose from the verandah edge as if the Henrys were expected to sit there.

"Run into the kitchen for chairs," said Bertha unable to bear the thought of the Henrys ranging themselves on the beds.

Katie and Jimmy brought the chairs at once aware of the urgency crashing through the doorway with them—only two as the children sat on stools to have their meals.

Horrie still had his hand on Hector's shoulder.

"Come in too, old son," he said as if Hector had suffered a bereavement, which in a sense was true looking at the Buick.

Horrie just about bounded up the steps with Hector following. He took one of the chairs and Mrs Henry the other and the daughters stood about not sitting on the beds to Bertha's relief.

"Is the kettle on the boil Bertha?" said Horrie and when she trotted past Hector he lifted mournful eyes to her and nodded.

In the kitchen Bertha paled as she stood by the table and nervously rubbed the surface wiped clean after she had finished her bread mixing. She looked at the shelf above the stove to a canister marked biscuits but it held only, as she well knew, a half empty packet of lettuce seed and some loose pumpkin seeds saved from a pumpkin Horrie liked which she intended planting,

There was also the last letter from her sister Myrtle in Queensland.

"Bertha!" called Horrie from the verandah.

"Coming!" said Bertha although she stood quite still pressing her hands to her waist.

In a moment she went out and stood shyly in the doorway avoiding Horrie's accusing eyes.

He sat with his back to a verandah post and his legs stretched in relaxed fashion along the edge.

Out on the roadside the Henry boys had parts of the engine spread out and they were already well covered in grease particularly their white shirts which appeared to be the chosen dress by poor farmers for the sea on a Sunday.

"Look at their shirts," said the elder Henry girl wise in domestic matters although only fifteen.

"I told them, didn't I tell them?" said Mr Henry to Mrs Henry who flung a fly away from her face with her hand and might have been flinging Hector off too.

"You can't tell young ones anything these days," said Horrie.

He laid his cigarette carefully on the verandah. "Not a thing can you tell 'em."

"I could be havin' me rest like I always do," said Hector with a glance at one of the beds which Mrs Went saw and resisted an impulse to move up and guard it.

"We been up since four," said Hector.

"Half past three," said one of the younger Henry girls called Isabel.

"We got up at ha' past three for this! I knew it!" said Hector so loud the boys heard and rose like two young trees newly sprouted and looked across to the verandah.

"You wouldn't want us to have any fun, would you?" Mickey called.

"Call that fun?" Hector called back. "Not my idea of fun!"

"What's your idea of fun?" called Mickey.

"Workin's his idea of fun," said Joe holding a spanner against his trousers and leaving a long greasy mark which caused Mrs Henry to flinch and the Henry girl to sorrowfully shake her head of dark brown curls.

"Ignore him," said Mickey to Joe and as if they were the ones with automation they dropped in the one motion onto their haunches and began to put the engine parts together.

"You're wasting your time like I told you in the first place!" Hector called out.

The Henry boys set their jaws and worked faster.

Horrie put his head back against the verandah post and smoked.

"When are we going to the sea?" piped up the smallest Henry girl.

"Never!" said Hector.

Mrs Henry fanned her face with her hand worrying now about the condition of the corned beef in the hamper strapped to the back of the car.

The Went children by this had dropped down onto the verandah edge so they were as before but because of the hour they did not expect to see any more cars on their way to the sea.

They thrust their feet among the geraniums and caught the leaves between their toes and in a little while Isabel and Elsie the youngest Henry slipped down and sat on spaces left.

"Take off your shoes and do this," said Katie.

"Don't you!" said Mrs Henry. "We might be going any minute."

Hector made a noise through his nose.

"Which way will we be goin'?" he said very loud for Mickey and Joe to hear. "We'll be headin' for home—walkin'."

"I must say I like me Sundays at home too," said Horrie careful to keep the end of his cigarette clear of his trouser knee.

The young Wents rustled the geraniums with a gentle whispering, slithering sound. They glanced at their father anticipating a reprimand but Horrie appeared to be smoking in utter content.

"What about dinner for us all, Bertha?" he said and Bertha put out a hand in time to stop herself from sinking onto a verandah bed.

"No, no," said Mrs Henry. "Ours is in the hamper."

"The butter will be running into everything," said Mary the big Henry girl.

"We might get going any minute," said Mrs Henry beating at the heat near her face.

"Weeks they spent on that damn thing," said Hector. "Weeks and weeks and weeks."

"We shoulda been grubbin' or fencin'," called Mickey who had stood for a moment and moved towards some shade. He drew a hand down the side of his face leaving a great grease streak. "He had to do a bit instead of sittin' on a log yellin' out his orders!"

Joe clamped the bonnet down.

"Now see what happens!" called Hector. "We all know what'll happen!"

"Leave them alone," said Mrs Henry. "The poor things in all the heat!"

Mickey and Joe stood a little away from the car not attempting to get in or gather up the tools.

Mrs Henry stood too.

"Will we all get in in case it goes?" she called.

The younger Henry girls jumped to the ground and ran and climbed in the back.

They arranged their features into a look of smugness just in case.

Mrs Henry left the verandah and halted in the gateway prepared to go forward or back depending on the action of the Buick.

"Come and see the crop of tomatoes I got down the back," said Horrie to Hector getting up and slapping the dust from the seat of his pants.

The young Wents looked towards their mother in astonishment. The vegetable garden was all her work.

Hector stood slowly but did not move.

The big Henry girl with a show of dignity walked down the verandah steps and stood between her mother and the car displaying a shade more optimism than Mrs Henry.

As if there was no need for a verbal agreement Joe wrapped the tools in a piece of hessian and flung them on the floor in the front and got in behind the wheel and Mickey went behind and gripped the rack holding the hamper.

Mrs Henry and Mary got in squeezing their arms to their sides and their legs together trying to shrink themselves to a lighter weight.

They strained forward, those on the back seat pushing at the front seat until Joe angrily flung them off with his shoulders.

The Buick moved but it was due to Mickey stretched almost horizontal grunting and straining sliding on the gravel.

"Come and help, you old bastard!" called Joe to the verandah.

"See the way they talk to me," said Hector sorrowfully to Horrie.

"Terrible, terrible," said Horrie. He tried but didn't succeed in being sorrowful too.

The Buick phut, phut, phutted then was silent, then phutted some more with a tinge of purpose. The phutting died away then started up again mixed with a roar. The Buick started to move hopped twice then charged forward and Mickey ran from behind, jumped on the running board and tore a door open nearly upsetting Joe's driving by falling half on top of him. The Henrys in the back helped straighten him up.

Hector leapt to life as if shot and went through the gate with his navy blue suit coat flying behind him. Horrie jumped to the ground bypassing the steps and went after him.

The Went children rose from the verandah edge and watched the old car rock about and swoop to the right and left then straighten up and move not too fast and with a certain air of sedation with Hector running hard behind and Horrie running too and not quite keeping up.

The Wents on the verandah were speechless until a bend took the car and the pursuers out of their view.

Seven year old Tommy spoke first.

"Our Dad's gone to the sea on a Sunday," he said and there was a little sorrow, some amazement and a lot of reverence in his voice.

But while they stared at the road trying to digest this and wondering why it all looked so empty without the

Henrys Horrie came around the bend trotting towards home as if he was a brumby broken away from the mob and aware of the best place to be after all.

He came through the gate looping the wire over the post.

"Gate swingin' open as usual," he said.

He looked up at Bertha.

"Must be our dinner time," he said.

"Not too long, love," said Bertha on the trot to the kitchen.

At the table Horrie helped himself to Bertha's tomatoes, lettuce and shallots and she passed him the vinegar and bread. When he had eaten some he held his knife and fork and shook his head several times while everyone waited.

"It's a wicked, wicked practice," he said swooping on his food again.

"A fine man like Hector Henry," he said, an emotional tremor in his voice. "Treated like that."

Errol sitting by his mother looking up at her. "But our Dad nearly went to the sea on a Sunday, didn't he Mum?" he said.

He was only five. No one paid much attention to him.

Text Classics

The Commandant
Jessica Anderson
Introduced by Carmen Callil

Homesickness
Murray Bail
Introduced by Peter Conrad

Sydney Bridge Upside Down
David Ballantyne
Introduced by Kate De Goldi

Bush Studies
Barbara Baynton
Introduced by Helen Garner

A Difficult Young Man
Martin Boyd
Introduced by Sonya Hartnett

The Cardboard Crown
Martin Boyd
Introduced by Brenda Niall

The Australian Ugliness
Robin Boyd
Introduced by Christos Tsiolkas

All the Green Year
Don Charlwood
Introduced by Michael McGirr

The Even More Complete
Book of Australian Verse
John Clarke
Introduced by John Clarke

Diary of a Bad Year
J. M. Coetzee
Introduced by Peter Goldsworthy

Wake in Fright
Kenneth Cook
Introduced by Peter Temple

The Dying Trade
Peter Corris
Introduced by Charles Waterstreet

They're a Weird Mob
Nino Culotta
Introduced by Jacinta Tynan

The Songs of a Sentimental Bloke
C. J. Dennis
Introduced by Jack Thompson

Careful, He Might Hear You
Sumner Locke Elliott
Introduced by Robyn Nevin

Terra Australis
Matthew Flinders
Introduced by Tim Flannery

My Brilliant Career
Miles Franklin
Introduced by Jennifer Byrne

The Fringe Dwellers
Nene Gare
Introduced by Melissa Lucashenko

Cosmo Cosmolino
Helen Garner
Introduced by Ramona Koval

Dark Places
Kate Grenville
Introduced by Louise Adler

The Long Prospect
Elizabeth Harrower
Introduced by Fiona McGregor

The Watch Tower
Elizabeth Harrower
Introduced by Joan London

The Mystery of a Hansom Cab
Fergus Hume
Introduced by Simon Caterson

The Glass Canoe
David Ireland
Introduced by Nicolas Rothwell

A Woman of the Future
David Ireland
Introduced by Kate Jennings

Eat Me
Linda Jaivin
Introduced by Krissy Kneen

The Jerilderie Letter
Ned Kelly
Introduced by Alex McDermott

Bring Larks and Heroes
Thomas Keneally
Introduced by Geordie Williamson

Strine
Afferbeck Lauder
Introduced by John Clarke

Stiff
Shane Maloney
Introduced by Lindsay Tanner

The Middle Parts of Fortune
Frederic Manning
Introduced by Simon Caterson

Selected Stories
Katherine Mansfield
Introduced by Emily Perkins

The Home Girls
Olga Masters
Introduced by Geordie Williamson

The Scarecrow
Ronald Hugh Morrieson
Introduced by Craig Sherborne

The Dig Tree
Sarah Murgatroyd
Introduced by Geoffrey Blainey

The Plains
Gerald Murnane
Introduced by Wayne Macauley

Life and Adventures 1776–1801
John Nicol
Introduced by Tim Flannery

Death in Brunswick
Boyd Oxlade
Introduced by Shane Maloney

Swords and Crowns and Rings
Ruth Park
Introduced by Alice Pung

Maurice Guest
Henry Handel Richardson
Introduced by Carmen Callil

The Getting of Wisdom
Henry Handel Richardson
Introduced by Germaine Greer

The Fortunes of Richard Mahony
Henry Handel Richardson
Introduced by Peter Craven

The Women in Black
Madeleine St John
Introduced by Bruce Beresford

An Iron Rose
Peter Temple
Introduced by Les Carlyon

1788
Watkin Tench
Introduced by Tim Flannery

Happy Valley
Patrick White
Introduced by Peter Craven